Billionaire Arranged Vows

An Enemies to Lovers Age Gap Romance

Sienna Adams

Awe Inspired Publications

Contents

Prologue

Avi

T HE LITTLE SPITFIRE SLAPPED me.

I didn't know what was more shocking, the way my head snapped back or the fact that my little goody-two-shoes wife actually got physical and slapped me.

One look at her furious face told me that I wouldn't be getting an apology any time soon either.

"I hope you have a reason for that, beautiful, because when I get my hands on you..." I stopped halfway through the warning, reminded once more how young my bride was when her eyes widened and then narrowed again.

In seconds her arms were folded under her full breasts, dragging my attention away from her eyes and back to the way her hips cocked out. "When you get your hands on me, you'll do what?"

If I had my way then she'd be laid out on the dining room table inside, panties dropped to her ankles while I smacked that ass of hers until it was a pretty pink like her cheeks. The little brat needed to be disciplined and my cock hardened at the very thought. I wouldn't even need to take her dress off, the silk looked loose enough that it could pool around that little dip in her waist while I took her.

No, I scrubbed my jaw. That wasn't going to happen. I had to stop thinking with my dick. She was too young. I needed to get a grip, hell maybe another drink wouldn't hurt. It would be better if I went inside before the little she-devil made me do something I really shouldn't be doing. Like her against the door of my car... My eyes unfocused as an image came to mind and I wondered if she'd glare when I put her on her knees for me. Those eyes of hers were danger-ous. Amber, like a wolf, and that long black hair of hers would look even better wrapped around my fist.

"You'll do what, Avi?" Alisha repeated through gritted teeth in a way that almost, almost sounded like a hiss, and fuck if that didn't make my pants tighten further. My name on her lips was the sweetest sound, no matter how angry she was when she said it. "What were you going to say, Avi?"

All thoughts of how wrong this was disappeared, and I took another good long look at how that dress hugged her curves. I'd pay a hundred grand just to see her wear dresses like that every time I got home. Cream silk with the thinnest straps on her shoulders. Thin enough to snap if I wanted to. I didn't really know why she was dressed up; it wasn't exactly casual wear not with the makeup and heels too. Were we supposed to be going somewhere?

"Avi!" she snarled, interrupting my thoughts and I couldn't resist smirking. Wonder what she'd say if I told her exactly how I was going to rip that dress off? I couldn't care how much it cost. I'd pull it down just to see her breasts sway without the material holding them up, and if that made her mad too then I'd buy her a dozen more. She wouldn't even need to sheath those pretty, manicured claws. I've never had any problem with my girls digging their fingernails into me.

"Nothing," I answered before turning back toward the little hunting cabin. There was a couch with my name on it, and if I was lucky then maybe some leftover bourbon too.

"Where are you going?" Alisha demanded, stomping behind me, and before I could even shut the door, her fingers were splayed wide against the wood, and it slammed back into the wall. "Avi! I swear to God if you don't answer me right now—"

So much for some peace and quiet. Whoever spilled the secret about the cabin better be praying to whichever deity they'd dedicated themselves to because I was going to put them through hell for this. I combed through my hair and pulled off my tie completely, throwing it onto the couch where a pillow and blanket were still crumpled from this morning. Was it too much to hope for one night's sleep in this place?

"Answer which question? You're going to need to be a little more specific, spitfire, I've barely had a chance to speak after all your accusations," I drawled, running my fingers through my hair again as I glanced over the dining room table. It was just tall enough and I sure as fuck was drunk enough that bending her over the glossy wooden surface seemed like a good idea. Except there were dishes on it; why the fuck?!

My mind was swimming, the alcohol in my bloodstream making it hard to remember what I'd been doing but then I did, and I let out a painful groan. Fucking paperwork. I was supposed to clear this shit out of here before going out. Moron.

"Why the hell are you sleeping here instead of in the house?" Alisha repeated each word slowly as if I didn't hear her the first time. The fucking impertinent little— *shit*. The papers. The last thing I needed was for her to see the divorce papers.

"You forget," I stated, turning to face her again. How the hell was I going to make her leave? The woman was like a one-woman army, and her wolf eyes were filled with so much suspicion. "This is my property, *wife*. Marrying me doesn't make it yours. I don't need to answer you."

Her eyes darkened and my *wife* took a step forward with that pretty little snarl on her lips. Good. Maybe if I pissed her off enough then she'd leave like she normally did. "Maybe you're the one forgetting, Avi, because the contract clearly stated that this relationship is monog-amous. If you're hiding up here just to fuck another woman then I won't need that stupid arrangement to make you regret that."

Where the hell did she come up with these things? Sometimes I wondered if this woman was fucking insane. How the fuck was I supposed to find someone else when the scent of her was invading fucking everything. My car. My house. My bed. Shit, even my suits were starting to smell like her. No matter where I went, all I could smell was a mixture of daisies and icy vanilla. There was no getting a break. My balls were so blue I was starting to worry they'd fall off. I scratched the scruff of my jaw. I just needed a little bit more patience and maybe another bourbon.

A growl from my bride interrupted my thoughts, and maybe if I hadn't finished off that last bit of Jack Daniels then I would've been more capable of handling how she was acting. Instead, my cock throbbed as Alisha grew irritated with my silence and whipped off her high heels only to throw them at me. Or tried to. I watched in amusement as they bounced in separate directions.

"You should work on your aim, spitfire," I smirked, regretting my words a second later when the little she-devil let out a shriek. I couldn't help my amusement, but I blamed Alisha for that too. She shouldn't be so interesting.

"Fuck you!" she yelled before spinning and walking off. Barefoot. In the forest.

I swore.

"Alisha!"

Chapter 1

Alisha

For some, one small act of kindness was enough. Sometimes all it took was a scarf on a cold day to keep away the chill, or an umbrella to survive a night in the rain. I'd seen it happen enough times to know. Yet no matter how many things I did for the women at the shelter, it never *felt* like enough.

To someone in their position, a life like mine was a fairytale, and yet one small contract and here I was acting like a spoiled brat in her favorite hiding place.

Being self-aware didn't make much difference though.

"What am I doing?" I whispered to the wind before tucking my legs under my chin.

Avi Zohran.

My eyes closed as I tried to imagine who the name belonged to. Was he young, or old? Rich? There was no question about it but what about his morals? How would he treat a woman like me, and would he expect me to change who I am to fit into his life? I wasn't religious but neither were the others but hadn't changed anything. I'd seen how Ava changed her life to become Christian like her husband and watched silently when Sierra gave up studying when she got pregnant. Everything for men that our parents practically sold them over to, and now they expected the same thing from me. The problem was that I couldn't see myself giving away parts of myself for another person, no matter what business they brought to the table.

A Google search would have stopped all my wondering, but I couldn't physically type his name out on my search bar. It wouldn't change anything anyway; money could erase the worst secrets. If that man was going to be my husband, then I'd determine what kind of person he was myself when I met him.

"Who are you, Avi Zohran?" I whispered with a sigh, stretching my legs and knocking my gold heels into the balcony railing. Up on the roof, with nothing but the stars and the roses yet not even my favorite place could stop that name from interrupting my peace.

Avi Zohran.

If I'd been at the shelter, I could have kept myself busy enough to forget that name and its significance. I could've cooked or cleaned. I could've seen who was showing up with bruises or hid behind clothes that were a little too baggy. If that didn't help, then it wouldn't be difficult to find something to do. There was always something that needed to be done, paperwork, cleaning, counseling, and that was just the tip of the iceberg. The shelter didn't have a chef on their payroll. Some months we didn't even make the rent. I should've been there to help instead of dressing in a silk gown I probably wouldn't ever wear again and sipping from a bottle of champagne that cost more than we'd raised at the charity drive last month. This whole situation was ridiculous.

The window squeaked and I glanced over before letting out a loud groan.

"Sunshine!" Talon crooned as he crawled onto the little rooftop ledge beside me. His eyes were dark and sparkling, and even from over here, I could smell the champagne on his breath.

"What are the chances? Guess we both got conned into being here tonight."

"Go away," I answered bluntly before turning my attention to my fingernails. The black polish was chipped, my rebellion in light of today's news. I guess they'd be staying like that for a while. It's not like anyone would notice, very few people ever looked at the finer details anyway.

"Don't tell me you're still angry," Talon teased, looking like trouble in a suit missing a tie, his indigo blue shirt's first few buttons undone, and his face reddened from either the champagne or dancing. Grandmother would kill him if she caught him in this state. "It was a small joke, don't hold it against me, Sunshine."

"Small joke, my foot," I snapped with a glare. "How am I supposed to show up to my next business meeting with a bright pink car? No one takes me seriously enough as is."

"I'll get it changed," he promised, a kicked-puppy expression on his face. He tugged his cell phone out of his pocket and pulled off his jacket, crumpling it beside himself as if it didn't cost more than most people's paychecks.

"If you're here to cause more trouble, then I'm warning you now. I'm not in the mood," I said flatly before returning to the scenery below.

Ignoring my coldness, Talon grabbed my tense shoulders and pulled me in for a hug. His fingers wrinkled the expensive dress in a way that would make Grandmother curse, but I found it hard to care when that small action soothed a little of the hurt beneath my ribs. "Sorry, Ali, I won't touch your car again."

My lips pursed. "Hmm."

I didn't believe him.

The champagne bottle next to me was nearly finished but I pulled it up anyway, snorting when Talon reached through the window to grab a similar bottle. Grandmother always said we were born under the same moon for a reason.

"Is the party going well?" I muttered to break the silence, but if Talon answered then I didn't hear it. Something yellow caught my attention, a daisy growing between the roof slates. Something that didn't belong somewhere the rain could wash it away.

I plucked it impulsively and twisted it in my fingers until the petals quivered. Roses would always be my favorite, but seeing a daisy on the rooftop made me smile.

On any other day, I would've been in the garden, watching the rose petals flutter in the evening breeze. I already knew it would be quieter, the waves would crash against the shore and my heart would calm until it matched its rhythm. Down there, I would be a gate away from walking barefoot on the sand of the private beach, but I'd also be within direct sight of everyone at the party.

As a child, any problem disappeared when I could escape to my grandmother's rose garden. And on the days it wasn't enough, I'd run barefoot out the gate until the waves reached my toes and pulled me back to myself. Back then I'd thought the story about her, and my grandfather was romantic, like a real-life fairytale. Back then I'd wished to be another bride wooed by whomever my family picked. Those thoughts all disappeared over the years as I was forced to watch my cousins go through the family tradition, each one turning to alcohol instead of the husbands who were chosen for them.

My mood darkened further, and I crushed the daisy before letting the breeze take away the crumpled flower. I shouldn't have thought about that, it just made me feel worse.

Besides me, Talon let me go and leaned against the balcony railing, humming along to whichever jazzy tune was being played. He closed his eyes, face upturned, and I laid my head on his shoulder, pulling my bottom lip between my teeth as I lost myself in my thoughts again.

Avi Zohran.

Was he signing his part of the marriage contract now? My copy would only be given after his signature was on the dotted line. That could take weeks, years even, but the second it happened then I had to make a choice. The same one all my sisters and cousins had to make. Marriage or freedom.

It wasn't much of a choice. My oldest sister, Kara had chosen freedom, and my father cut her off without a second glance. I didn't even know where she was now. We weren't allowed to stay in touch, but the private investigators I hired on the side still let me know she was well every now and then. As well as anyone could be after losing their life with one decision, and now it was my turn.

Either I'd have to sacrifice my inheritance or spend the next seven years married to a stranger. Unless I ended up with a man like Aunt Lena had. One who preferred using his fists instead of his words. The thought made me grimace. That was the last thing I wanted. Still, freedom... or marriage? Seven years for my inheritance? Or my freedom for the price of every woman relying on the shelter?

I should've had more time. Chrysalis wasn't in the right place right now, we were supposed to have a few more years to get everything sorted. That's why I rushed graduation. That's why I worked so much harder to get my degree and start working for myself. I had a *plan.* I used to have a plan... there was supposed to be more time, it was almost suspicious how fast this deal was happening and along with *his* name running through my mind, there was another much more somber question. *Why now?*

"It's really not that bad, you know," Tal informed me eventually and my lips twitched at the irony of his words. He was referring to the party, no one would know about the arrangement until after I had decided and that would only come after my father let me know. He just hadn't realized his lawyer had more loyalty to me than him. He should've known better; I was an Altaha after all.

"If Mom's distracted then we can dance for a little while," Talon gestured, pulling me away from my thoughts again. There was a twinkle in his eyes that spelled mischief and I kept a wary eye on him. "Maybe grab some more champagne. I know I'm not the only one running low."

I forgot I was still holding my own bottle, but I didn't need to give it a swish to know that the contents inside were all finished. When I stole it, the sky had only just started setting. That must've been hours ago because the night had crept in and the stars above me mocked me with the cheerful twinkle.

"What are you doing out here anyway?" I asked instead, giving up on my musings for the remainder of the night. "Did Grandmother catch you with a caterer again?" I hid a grin when Talon repeated my words mockingly, pulling faces that could've landed him in trouble if Grandmother found out.

"You know, sometimes I forget how immature you are for your age but then you go and do things like that," I teased, hands on my hips. "Imagine what Grandmother would say? *Talon, think about your wife one day, mm?*"

He stopped long enough to give me the evil eye. "You wouldn't."

My eyebrows raised in return. "No?"

We both knew that I would, and had, told on Tal before. He'd been born much later than the rest of his siblings, and while it was horrifying to know that my grandparents still had enough sex to suffer a broken condom at their age, I don't know what I would've done without him. He was more a brother than an uncle with all the trouble we'd gotten up to.

"Nope," Talon grinned, wagging a finger in front of my line of sight. "You wouldn't dare ruin her night like that."

"Her night or yours," I snorted, Grandmother had never shied away from scolding any of us in public before. "How much longer do you think this one will last? My feet are killing me."

Grandmother had somehow persuaded over twenty up-and-coming artists to not only showcase their art but also sell it with the pro-ceeds going to her charities. Each was given a commission that cost more than the diamonds on my necklace to create ten pieces to be sold tonight. Grudgingly, I admitted that she knew how to play the game well. I'd never been able to pull this sort of shindig off.

"Sourpuss," Talon snickered, and I huffed. He wasn't the one who'd had to wear heels for more than ten hours. If I'd been in the shelter's kitchen, or even serving, I could have worn something more comfortable than the scarlet silk that imprisoned me, cutting off most movement unless I wanted to scandalize the elders in my family.

"Wonder what those old biddies will do if we put on some Doja Cat and paint the town red?" Tal said, wiggling his eyebrows until I snorted, imagining the shock on those women's faces. Seeing my amusement, he only continued. "Come on, I'm bored, Ali. Let's steal some Dom Perignon and snacks. Maybe we can hijack a laptop from the staff and come back to watch movies. Or... you know what? Dancing isn't a bad idea. Maybe we can teach them some new moves."

My laughter spilled out of me before I could contain it, and I didn't hesitate before allowing Talon to drag me back to the party. Joking aside, he didn't force me to twerk in front of Grandfather's associates, but he did get his way and somehow pulled me into a salsa that somehow had my tight red skirt twirling around me. We danced around the couples swaying in place until I saw Grandmother walking up the stairs and onto the small platform her band was playing on.

She held a hand out delicately to the band and grabbed a microphone, stopping me, and Talon by association, in place.

"I want to thank you all," Grandmother said into the microphone. Her voice was clear despite her age, and like it was planned, all the dancers stilled, and the room waited in anticipation to hear what she'd say next. Gran was known for her extravagance, but her flair for theatrics kept the guests entertained.

She smiled, a slight curl of the lips that didn't show nearly as much of her excitement as her dark eyes did. "As you know, this charity is one that I hold very close to my heart. I've spent years establishing it to the point where it is currently. Where we can provide opportunities to people who would never have had a chance otherwise. The Altaha scholarship was created in the hopes that it will allow many young people to become something greater when they wouldn't have had the chance otherwise."

She paused, her gracefully lined face turning down. "Not everyone has the financial stability to afford a tertiary education and as a country, we have been missing out on many intelligent people becoming doctors... scientists ... and artists like those who have decorated my ballroom with these magnificent pieces. So, for those who do not have the economic means, all your contributions will help us provide many students with life-changing opportunities, and for that, there is very little that could truly justify how grateful I—"

My cell phone started to ring, and I stopped listening to pull it out of the small gold clutch I'd been given. Grandmother's speech became little more than a distant noise when I read the name on the screen.

"I've got to take this," I murmured in Talon's ear, and he nodded distractedly, his eyes on a pretty blonde girl on the opposite side of the room.

Stepping out of the ballroom and toward the gardens, I answered in a whisper, "Please tell me you have some good news?"

On the other side of the line, my aunt let out a sigh. "Sorry, little bird, I'm afraid I don't."

My feet stilled on the grass, heels sinking in despite how time had frozen within me. One stuttered breath later, I found myself moving toward the gate at the edge of the garden. Silence and then, "Alisha?"

"I'm here," I murmured, stepping out of my heels and not bothering to pick them up. I walked on the crunchy sand, feeling my skirt tug behind me.

"He's signed the contract, sweetheart," Lena said a second before the waves washed across my bare feet. I sank onto the beach, not caring that my dress was getting wet.

Chapter 2

Alisha

I WOKE THE NEXT morning with almost no recollection after that conversation with Lena. There were flashes of sobbing, and a moment I remembered staring at my steering wheel, but I couldn't remember the rest. The pounding in my head felt like a hangover but when and with what alcohol? Did I go back to the house and steal more? Or did I come home and get wasted on my couch?

The buzzing of my cell phone displaced all those questions, and I muffled a groan before stretching my hand out to find it under my pillow. At some point, I must have walked my waterlogged behind back to my SUV and driven it home because I recognized the soft silky comforter I was laying across as my own.

Peering through one swollen eye to see who was calling, I grimaced.

Dad.

Oh, for crying out loud.

I had no choice but to answer, he didn't know that Lena was feeding me information and I couldn't jeopardize her firm when she was the only one making sure I, and all the other girls, were safe.

Whining into my pillow, I swiped on the screen and brought the phone to my ear.

"Good morning, little bird," Dad greeted cheerfully before I could say anything. "I heard you and Talon stole the show last night. Did you sleep well?"

"Of course!" I kept my tone light. "But I wouldn't say that we stole the show, you know nobody throws a party like Gran."

He let out a chuckle, "True. I'm sorry I couldn't make it. Your mother wasn't too happy with me, but we had a business arrangement to sort out first." My heart throbbed. A business arrangement, that's all I was at the end of the day. "Actually, that's why I'm calling. I have something that I need to discuss with you. What do you say I pick you up and we grab some breakfast at Cindy's?"

My stomach rolled at the idea of eating something, and I muffled a whimper, trying to think of an excuse while the world around me spun on its axis.

"Sorry, Dad, I'd love to, but I had a smoothie earlier..." I trailed off, scrubbing my face with my free hand while I looked around for any indication of the time. The TV was off, but the clock beside my bed said 08:49.

"A smoothie?" he repeated with a laugh. "Since when would you choose a smoothie over waffles?"

Since you want to speak to me about signing my freedom away, I glared at the floor, unable to think of anything else I could say to give me some more time.

"Oh, you know how it is, the girls had this new diet..." I lied again.

"Alright, alright," he chuckled. "Enjoy your smoothie, little bird, but then do you think you'll be able to meet me at the office in an hour?" It wasn't like I had a choice.

"Sure," I answered quietly, my eyes burning as I stared into space. Wedding bells tolled in my mind like a death march. "I'll meet you there at ten o'clock."

꒰꒱ ⋆ ꒰꒱

Forty minutes later, I stood outside my car and swore. It was *pink*.

"Damn it, Talon!"

I don't know how I forgot about his stupid prank. I pressed the bottom of my palms to my closed eyes and tried to think of a way out of this. My father's office was twenty minutes away, and I should've left already. I was already late even though a full hour hadn't already passed.

"I can't go to the meeting with that," I groaned, imagining everyone's faces when I pulled up in my bubblegum pink SUV. Yet there wasn't enough time to fix it so after cursing Talon again, I got in and buckled my seatbelt. "I'm going to kill him this time, I swear to god."

Lena phoned as I pulled out of the undercover garage; she didn't even spare me a greeting before she asked if I was on the way. Despite the past hour of building myself up, my breath still hitched at the reminder. "I'm on the road now but I'll probably be there in about ten or twenty minutes."

Silence reigned before the Bluetooth speaker crackled from her sigh. "I wish I could change this for you, little bird, but I can't."

"I know," I whispered loud enough for her to hear. My fingers clenched on the steering wheel before relaxing. "Just— just tell me what you found out."

Her response was quiet, an indication she was at the office. "Not much I'm afraid. I only managed to get the bare minimum. You know as well as I do that there isn't much information that can come from a background search. If you want to know if he has a criminal record, well he doesn't but that doesn't mean much."

I knew that. *God*, I knew that.

"What *do* you know?" I asked instead.

There were so many questions running through my mind. I didn't know where he'd been born, or how old he was. He could've been my age, or maybe he was older, with children. Would I have a problem with step kids? And what about his family? I didn't know if he had siblings or if he was an only child. Had he gone to college? Did he have a job? Knowledge was power and my husband-to-be had all of it. All of the men chosen to marry one of us were given a portfolio on what they'd be getting, and

I knew mine would list everything my parents were aware of. My medical information, my age, and possibly even my body description. My MBA, my charity, and even a few of my hobbies. There was very little on those papers that they wouldn't know. Which meant there was little *he* wouldn't know too.

Another sigh crackled my car's speakers. "Avi Zohran is thirty-two years old," *nine years older than me.* "And has only one living relative I can find on the system. There is almost no knowledge about his mother, besides a name. Bella Hayes. It's almost like she's a ghost."

Or maybe she was just another victim of the rich and famous. My mouth set in a grim line as Lena continued. "William Zohran, his father, was killed in a car accident approximately three months before his birth. Heaven knows what happened during that time but a year later we've got a record of Avi being in his grandfather's care. He was linked as a primary guardian after taking his grandson in for vaccinations at a hospital near their family home."

I felt numb as I processed this information. I didn't want to feel sympathy for my soon-to-be husband, but his childhood sounded lonely. His mother's disappearance was suspicious though.

What would make someone disappear so thoroughly that not even Lena's systems could pick up on her?

"Is there anything else?" I asked softly, hoping to hear more. I was only a few streets away from the office, meaning we had less time than I'd hoped to go over everything.

Lena hummed under her breath. "Some general information, yes. Avi is the CEO of Zohran Tech, a family business that specializes in leading security software and is currently trying to branch out into the direction of AI-operated medical equipment and software. They're currently the leading competitor in several fields, but those two came up the most in all my searches. The technology they're proposing to bring into the medical world is almost unheard of and will be worth billions if they get it right. According to the media, a source close to them spilled the news that Zohran Tech is working on an artificially intelligent system that can assist doctors in operating on high-risk patients. I don't have all the details, but it looks like it is meant to monitor the vitals of a patient being operated on and will have the ability to stabilize them without having too many hands in an operating room. It will work as a second pair of eyes, as well as alerting the doctors to any specific patterns that they might have missed in the patient's health history. Avi seems to be in charge of the project. He's been the media's favorite little genius since he took his first steps as CEO at twenty-three, but his grandfather only stepped down after Avi's thirtieth birthday."

"Holy shit," I whispered as I pulled the car into the office parking lot. I turned the car off and slumped into my seat. So, he wasn't just anybody, he was someone the media knew, someone in charge of a billion-dollar company. That made him powerful, and that meant that I had more of a disadvantage than I'd initially realized.

"I'll be there the entire time," Lena reassured but it wasn't enough. My body was trembling as I grabbed my handbag off the passenger seat.

"Ali?"

A sob trapped the words in my throat, and I squeezed my eyes shut in a hopeless attempt to stop the tears.

"Alisha, snap out of it. I can practically hear your thoughts from here," Lena growled. Watching the glass doors of my father's company, I saw her step out and fold her arms. "Look at me, Alisha."

I did, and through my blurry vision, I fought a sob. Even through the blur, I could see the burns running up and down both her arms. The parts left uncovered by her sleeveless, turtle-neck dress.

"What happened to me won't ever, *ever* happen to you. Do you hear me? This contract is tight, I've had my best associates look at it before sending it through," Lena stated calmly until my breath evened. "Talon and I will be a phone call away if anything happens. You know that. Now take a deep breath and straighten your spine. I won't let anyone hurt you, and besides... You're an Altaha."

"Okay," I sniffed, lowering the mirror to check my eyes before I muttered it again. Almost as if to reassure myself.

I am an Altaha. Those words used to bring me comfort, but not anymore. Now they were an obligation of a tradition spanning generations. The Altaha name didn't have the honor that it used to, the power that my family had curated was built upon marriage agreements. Every woman, and sometimes the men too, were given this choice.

I took a deep breath and gathered my things. I could do this. I had to, if not for myself then for

Chrysalis. I got out of the car and walked toward the front doors that Lena held open. She gave me a comforting smile, yet my shoulders only pulled from my ears once she walked beside me. Every step next to her side gave me more confidence, and I locked that scared little girl away, straightening my shoulders second by second. Our family had gone a long way from the tribe that it once was, but staying in the city didn't change the fact that we were once warriors.

The elevator mirrors showed us side by side as we entered, and the burn marks on her arms taunted me once more. Unlike the rest of the wives, Lena wasn't beholden to family traditions. Still, those pink burns on her olive skin felt like a warning. I knew the story well, although I was only twelve when it happened. I just didn't know how. That was a secret *my* family had paid to keep. All we knew was that there was a house fire and she managed to escape, dragging her broken body to the nearest hospital. It was ruled an accident, and nobody dared to question the fact that her abusive husband was dead. Those were the kinds of things that money hid, and although I'd seen the scars a thousand times over the years, today was the first time, I truly understood the gravity of this contract.

A moment before the elevator beeped, Lena turned to me and murmured. "Do me a favor?"

I raised a single eyebrow in question. There wasn't much I'd be able to do to help with the negotiation that was coming.

"Don't treat your future like it's my past," she said, her eyes a shade of honey darker than mine. "Sometimes, and I'm not saying now is the case, but sometimes when we believe something will be bad then that's the outcome we're given. I've done everything to grant you the protection I didn't have. You will be safe, but only you can decide if you'll be happy. Seven years is a long time to live with someone you hate."

With those words, the elevator beeped, and the doors opened. I ran my sweaty palms down my skirt before we stepped out and walked toward my father's office. A breath later, we stood in front of the wooden door, and I had seconds to steel myself before Lena opened it, and I came face to face with my future husband.

Five men were waiting when we walked in and the fear, I'd been feeling a moment ago came back twice as strong when I saw my grandfather sitting amongst them.

What the hell was he doing here? I glanced at Lena with wide eyes. My grandfather hadn't dealt with these *arrangements* since her generation. He stepped down after Lena's marriage. That was the rule, so why was he here now?

Stop panicking, Lena's glare said, and I bit my lip as I turned back to the men. I didn't recognize the other three, but the one closest to me glanced up with a friendly grin and eyes that were gray and curious.

I met his grin with one of my own, even though it was a brittle double, and looked at the man beside him. He had dark hair, olive skin, and tattoos that curled on his arms. Familiar markings. Navajo markings. I'd notice them anywhere because most of the men in our family had the same. His face was hawkish and stern as he looked me over but there wasn't enough interest in them, so I ignored him to look at the man at the edge of the table.

Blue-gray eyes met mine and my breath hitched. Him. I would place a bet on my life that the man with blue-gray eyes was Avi Zohran.

He didn't look anything like the tech genius I'd imagined.

Those sharp blue eyes broke our gaze and scanned me almost lazily while my heart thudded in my chest. His shoulders might have been relaxed and his face bored but that was all meant to deceive. Those eyes were calculating and vivid in a way that the rest of his face wasn't. His features were light but not colorless, his hair a short, rich brown that barely fell over his eyebrows, and to seal the deal? High cheekbones and lips with the perfect cupid's bow.

I'd seen enough beautiful men not to be intimidated by appearances. Yet something in that expression of his made my feet shift and my stomach twist. For the first time, I felt like the little bird they all called me. A silly little bird trying to be a hunter instead of the hunted, and if Avi was anything, then it was the cat doing the hunting.

When those blue eyes met mine again, the disinterest turned my nerves to irritation and when he turned to face Grandfather, effectively dismissing me, I bristled.

My eyes narrowed briefly, what an asshole.

"There you both are," Dad said, and I broke my stare with a blink. *What am I doing?* I relaxed my shoulders and attempted to control my reactions, but it was too late. Amusement curled my betrothed's lips. A catlike grin that didn't go unnoticed if Lena's stiffened shoulders implied anything. Out of the both of us, Lena was the better actress, so I wasn't surprised when her tension disappeared a second later.

"Sorry about being late," she said with a flick of her hair. The smile on her face was more polite than friendly, but Lena approached the men with steadier steps than I would have as she walked straight up to Avi and held out her hand.

"Mr. Zohran, I presume?" she didn't wait for him to answer before continuing. "It's a pleasure. I'm Lena Altaha. I've been dealing with your lawyers."

Avi rose from the chair with a cool expression before taking her palm in his. His eyes held hers for a moment before meeting mine again and for a second, it felt like he was speaking to me and not her. "The pleasure is all mine."

His voice was a smooth timber that left me with goosebumps, and I swallowed the longer he stared. I didn't dare look away, but I wouldn't hesitate to admit that I preferred when he pretended to be disinterested. Butterflies danced in my stomach and a dark eyebrow raised thoughtfully before he broke his gaze and turned back to Lena with a charming grin. "I've heard a lot about your prowess as a lawyer."

I had to hold my breath to stop myself from sighing in relief, but it wouldn't have mattered anyway because my whole body stiffened again a moment later when he held his hand out for me. "Alisha Altaha, I presume?"

"That's right." I subtly wiped my palm on my skirt before offering it to him. Avi shook my hand and then let go, tipping his head in the direction of the blonde-haired man. "These are my associates. My lawyer, Silas Goodwin," Silas grinned, his gray eyes kind as she stood up to shake Lena's hand. I held out my own for the same introduction and then turned toward the tattooed man next to them, "and my head of security, Kai Adakai."

Kai dipped his head but that was all the acknowledgment he gave before Grandfather rose from his leather chair and straightened his suit.

"Wonderful! That makes things a little easier," Grandfather boomed and even without looking, I could hear the smile in his voice. In my periphery, I watched him pull out a chair and gesture for Lena to sit. Then he pulled out another and I thanked God that my legs were steady as I slowly moved toward it. "Alisha, I'm excited to announce that the reason we wanted to meet with you this morning is to discuss your marriage arrangement with Avi."

Grandfather placed a heavy hand on my shoulder that I fought not to throw off. "My marriage agreement?" I echoed with a smile that felt fragile as I stared across the table at my father. That wasn't a lie, but I couldn't control the way my voice hardened as I continued. "I thought I had another few years."

I felt more than saw the men shift in their seats as my grandfather's hand tightened. It wasn't a lie though. Unlike the rest of my cousins and aunts, I was a good few years younger than any other *bride*. Still, I couldn't let them know that I already knew so I softened my voice in the hopes it would sound pleading. "Dad, don't you think this is a bit soon?"

In the time it took him to respond, my heart slowed to a stop. He couldn't know that Lena had been helping me, otherwise, it wouldn't take much to find out everything she'd done for the other girls as well. Maybe I was wrong. Maybe defiance wasn't the answer. Then again, how was a girl supposed to act when she was given the news her marriage had been decided?

"I was told that my future wife would be aware of these plans," Avi said coolly, and I peeked at him to see the cold expression on his face. It suited him far better than that blank mask he'd worn earlier.

Grandfather finally let out a laugh. "Ah, you're right. You're right. I should've said something sooner. Please do forgive me, gentlemen. It's tradition to let the bride-to-be know before the contract gets signed; unfortunately, though, with how quickly you wanted this meeting, I couldn't do that."

That little detail he'd let slip told me a lot more than he thought, and I peered at Avi as Grandfather walked back to his seat. So, he needed a bride soon then, did he? I could use that as leverage for the contract. My eyes met Lena's as I placed my bag in the seat beside me.

"Forgive me," I echoed, and I purposefully softened my features as I glanced around. "I'm just surprised."

"Of course," Avi replied quietly, but his eyes were hard when they turned toward Grandfather. "I suppose that means that this meeting will be to discuss the contract then?"

"Correct. Rest assured, the women in our family have as much choice in the marriage as their suitors do. Each is given two weeks to decide on whether they accept the terms provided," Grandfather informed him before turning toward me and adding in unnecessarily. "Unless you choose to sign the documents today, that is."

I nodded; I understood the terms. He didn't have to repeat it.

Dad motioned toward the papers in Silas' hands. "Lena, please go ahead."

Underneath the table, her hand squeezed mine quickly before she let go to pick up the papers that Silas pushed her way. Lena flicked through them before turning toward me to explain. "Alisha, I've personally prepared your contract with Mr. Zohran. Most of the terms you will be familiar with, such as the agreement that you will be married to him for seven years. However, there is more that has been requested which you will need to approve before signing it."

"Such as?" I said, keeping my tone light. Lena wouldn't allow the men to take advantage.

Her eyes met mine, steady as always, and I saw pride in the way I was handling the situation. Even with that though, there was a foreboding pinch at the corner of her mouth that told me I wouldn't like what had been added. "An heir will need to be provided before the end of the year."

An heir.

A *baby*.

My face flushed as my eyes swung toward my Avi. Was that why this arrangement was so rushed? Why the hell did he need an heir? Dear god, I hadn't even come to terms that I'd be marrying him, and they were already stating that sex was a requirement!

"An heir," I echoed stupidly. What reasons would a man like him need an heir? Unless... was there something wrong with him? I blanked my expression. If Avi Zohran was dying, then that meant I wouldn't have to face the full seven-year term.

Avi was silent on the other side of the table, his eyes sharp as shards of ice when I met them. Could I have sex with a man like that? Avi was built like a bear with strong shoulders and an athlete's frame but those eyes... I had a feeling that a man like that could ruin me.

"Alisha?" Lena prodded, and I glanced back at her, feeling more nervous than before. "Would you like me to read the rest of the agreement?"

"Y-yes."

Lena nodded, but as she read, she looked at me with the same expression as in the elevator. I knew what she wanted. I had to get it together. Dear god, I had to get it together.

With one last look at Avi, I took a deep breath and listened to Lena speak. She ran over the rest of the details. Easy things, normal per what I knew of the other girls' contracts. And more in line with what she told me when we walked into the building. My inheritance would be fully handed over at the end of the seven-year trial, but I would be allowed to use twenty percent a year until that time. I had to move in with my husband and live on his property for the first two years. The wedding would take place exactly a month after I signed the contract, but the announcement would happen in a week... etc., etc., etc. but I got stuck at the last bit.

"Sorry, what was that?" I interrupted, begging her to repeat what I wasn't sure she'd said. I had to have dreamed it because it almost sounded like she said—

"You'll be required to work at Zohran Tech for the first two years of your marriage," Lena repeated with a barely concealed wince. "For four to five days a week."

"What about my business?" I demanded, furiously glancing at my grandfather and Avi. I knew he would've told Avi about it. It would've been in the documents provided as well as everything else about me that my parents knew. "The organization demands my time. How am I expected to run it while catering to these requirements? We aren't at the point yet where I can bring another person on to do what I'm doing and besides that... what could you possibly need me to do while working at Zohran Tech?"

"You'll be my assistant." Avi met my eyes without blinking, and I gaped at him.

"Your assistant!" I sputtered, digging my fingers into the arms of the chair. The very idea was insulting. To have to run around after my husband like some sort of... I ground my teeth. "I didn't realize that this was a job interview, and even if it were, I already have a business to look after."

"A business that wouldn't be standing without your inheritance," my grandfather reminded me bluntly.

Fuck. That was the problem, wasn't it? Everyone in the family could spout poetic about our choices but in this, I had none. My eyes squeezed shut as I drew in a breath and turned to Lena. "What else is in the contract that I need to be made aware of?"

"We've gone over the most important," she advised, and I nodded, glancing at the pen next to her hand. I didn't have any choice in this marriage. Not if I still wanted to keep Chrysalis. Still though, very little in that contract benefitted me. I couldn't be the only one losing out. That wasn't fair, and I refused to give up seven years of my life without getting something out of it. Something besides my inheritance.

My chin raised in defiance as I looked at my husband-to-be. "I'll agree to your terms, but on one condition."

Avi's eyebrow raised, but he motioned for me to continue.

"I won't work there for a full working week. That wouldn't be fair to my current obligations. I'll work there for two days, that's all I'm willing to give and in return, I expect the same from you. For every day that I work at Zohran Tech, you will give the same amount of time to Chrysalis."

Amusement glinted in those blue depths as Avi stared at me with the same intensity that I looked at him. I didn't drop my gaze and eventually, he nodded sharply, just once, but it was enough.

"Smart girl, but unfortunately, I don't have the time available to put into a non-profit. However, I'll agree to change the terms to *three* days, and I'll pay for you to have an assistant of your own for the charity."

I glanced at Lena, and the look on her face said I wouldn't get a better deal out of it. Looking at my father and grandfather nearly made me flinch. Their dark eyes were hard, and it was clear they were running out of patience.

"I'll sign it."

Chapter 3

Avi

M Y SHOULDERS WERE TIGHT after hearing Alisha Altaha's declaration. After all the preparation, I didn't actually expect this to go ahead. Her lower lip was caught between her teeth but even still, I could see the slightest tremble. Disgust curdled my stomach the same way it had when she'd walked into the room with those dark eyes of hers blown wide with terror.

This was wrong.

It didn't take a genius to see that Altaha's granddaughter didn't have a choice in this arrangement. The lack of surprise only worsened it all. I heard that these sorts of arrangements were normal for Tao Altaha, but hearing the rumors and seeing them proven were two different things, and I didn't want to be another chess piece for a man like him to play with.

Worse though, I didn't want the girl across from me to be one either. She was too young for this bullshit, and I should've tried harder to get out of this deal, but I couldn't risk the deal with Bourgetti to get out of this agreement.

What surprised me most of all was that his son was just as content signing away his youngest daughter, as Tao was. Rowen Altaha had negotiated most of the terms on behalf of his daughter, only giving the contract to his sister, Lena, after we'd discussed it.

A vibration in my pocket pulled my attention to my cell phone and I pulled it out to glance at the screen, masking my features before they gave away what I was thinking.

Si [10:15]: *You look like you're going to vomit.*

With every twist of my stomach, it felt that way too.

My eyes dragged back to the girl in front of me. Grandfather wanted an heir, and it had to be hers but fuck, she was only twenty-three. Women at that age didn't want to settle down and have babies, they wanted independence and being spoiled. I couldn't afford the distraction of a young wife. I didn't have the time or capacity to give her the kind of life she needed, nor the motivation to get her to stop cold-shouldering me long enough to get her pregnant and barefoot in the kitchen.

Biting back a sigh, I typed a quick *fuck you* and settled back to study the women as they discussed certain parts of the agreement. Lena Altaha was a fucking good lawyer; good enough that I wanted her on my retainer, but that didn't mean she wasn't any less prone to avoiding the subject at hand. Hell, if the two of them carried on like this then I'd end up missing the meetings scheduled for today.

I cleared my throat before standing up, ignoring the girl's stare as I fixed my tie. "If you'll excuse me and my associates, we have a meeting in the next thirty minutes. Please ensure that there is a copy of the amended contract sent to me within the hour for me to sign." I just wanted to get this over with.

My voice was flat, maybe ruder than it should've been considering the preparation it took to get this arrangement, but I found it difficult to give either Rowan or Tao the kind of respect their family had acquired.

"Of course," Lena intercepted, plucking up the contract along with the notes she made. "I'll ensure my assistant sends a copy to all the parties involved."

"No," Tao interrupted with a sharp look her way. "I want you to give it to them personally."

Fire flashed in his daughter's eyes, but Rowan was quick to aid with an easy grin and a clap of his hands. Too bad his eyes were just as cold when he stood up from his chair. Satisfaction curled within me. Good. My insult was recognized then. "That leaves only the wedding arrangements then."

I raised an eyebrow and tried not to sneer. "You do have staff for that don't you?"

Tao's face grew colder, a good sign that I was pushing the boundaries, but fuck, I couldn't help it when he was doing this to *her*.

"It's in the contract," Lena supplied unhelpfully, and maybe a little unhappily too unless I was imagining the twist of her lips before her blank expression met my stare head-on. "The wedding preparation is left with the husband to ensure that the brides are married in the culture of their new families."

That was the last straw. Kai's whispered *what the fuck* was loud enough for me to hear and this time I didn't hide the sneer before turning toward Rowan Altaha. "I don't have time for wedding preparations. Let the girl choose what she wants, and we'll go with that."

"I'm afraid that's not possible, Mr. Zohran," Lena answered smoothly while her father and brother bristled. "The contract dictates that the groom is responsible for the wedding. However, if your schedule can't accommodate this, then you are welcome to arrange a wedding planner to assist with the finer details."

My jaw clicked as I gritted my teeth, my eyes straying to the girl again. They weren't even giving her a choice.

Surprisingly, she was looking straight at me, her eyes filled with fire. And here I'd been thinking she was nothing more than a pushover by signing that contract without taking the full two weeks to consider it.

Turning once more toward Tao and Rowan, I stated, "Thank you, but I'm not interested. If you'd like to discuss anything further, you're welcome to reach out but I've got to go."

After one more glance at my new bride, I walked out.

"Silas, you better find me a way out of this fucking contract," I warned the moment we got into the car. My fingers clenched around the steering wheel, and my foot pushed down on the gas as I pulled out of the parking lot.

"My team's looked at everything," he replied as he scratched at his jaw. "Unfortunately, it looks like your grandfather has everything locked down tight. Without an heir, the company automatically goes to your cousin."

I swore, slamming on brakes at the stop street and speeding up again as soon as I got onto the highway. If Aaric inherited the company, then we were all fucked. He couldn't run anything beyond the petty crimes that got him locked up a few years ago. This seemed to be the only thing my grandfather and I could agree on.

"Fuck it," I cussed again, shaking my head at the thought. There was no use thinking about that. "Any news on the leak, at least?"

In the last week, we'd had several leaks go out to the press about the model of our newest piece of technology, as well as the software it was using. The board of directors was furious, and of course, the blame was on me.

"Nothing, but we've gotten rid of any loose ends on the project, and the staff are each going through a vicious screening process to make sure no one has their cell phones on site," Kai reported before going quiet. "There has to be something that we're missing here. This is the second time now that software intel has been leaked."

"The first time was to ForTech, and we fired the data processor for selling us out," Silas commented. "Can I recommend we stall our internships until it's done? Maybe the leak isn't on the team but rather kids hoping to score with a higher internship elsewhere."

It wasn't a bad idea; in fact, I could name a few of our competitors who would pay a better price for any intern who gave them one of our company secrets during their interviews.

My fingers tapped on the steering wheel before I gave a short nod. "That's fine. We have enough staff on hand to complete the current set of trials for the project. Get on a call with Human Resources and let them know the plan. Make sure the publicity team is on this as well. We don't want to lose our partnerships with the universities, so tell them to spin something that won't get us into trouble."

"It might be best to involve the legal team too," Si mentioned, tapping one fingertip casually against his knee. A tell he'd had since our college days, one that told me his mind was busy.

"If we need the legal team, then use them." The car roared as I accelerated, and a smile curved my lips. "ForTech isn't going to get their hands on this patent. Make sure of that."

"A distraction might help with that," Kai commented, and my grin fell again. I already knew what type of distraction he meant.

"No," the warning was spoken through gritted teeth as my fingers clenched on the steering wheel again.

"I don't know, Avi, it might actually be just what we need to throw ForTech off our trail," Si agreed, glancing at me warily.

Fuck that.

"The plan is to get out of this fucked up deal, not to encourage it," I bit out.

"And if you can't?" Si raised an eyebrow at me. "The last thing you want to do is offend your grandfather or the Altahas. The attention it will bring could ruin everything. My suggestion is to roll with it. Let the public know their favorite playboy is off the market, and if we can break the contract, then you can make some excuse saying that it didn't work out."

"And then what?" I snapped, pushing the car a little faster until Si's hand creaked on the door handle. I heard him call me an asshole under his breath and grinned. He was fine with speed when he drove but let it be anyone else and he'd throw a hissy fit.

"No doubt they've already amended and gotten the girl to sign the updated contract," Kai reminded me, and I looked in the rearview mirror in time to see him leaning comfortably against the seat. "You're practically married at this point so you might as well get used to it."

"No, I'm going to find a way out of it. There has to be a loophole."

"There might not be," Silas said, playing with his phone again. "But if there is, then it's going to take a long time to figure it out. You've only got four weeks. The best thing to do would be to play along with it. Hire a wedding planner to iron out the finer details for the moment. From what I could see, they weren't even that bothered about an engagement party, so you won't need to see your bride again until the wedding."

"You're both telling me to go along with it. She's twenty-three, that's younger than your sister, Si," I bit out. "What would you do in that case?"

Silas rubbed his face, thinking it over. "I'd think about how this is affecting her. You're right. She's twenty-three, but she's been told this would happen since she was in diapers. It's a family tradition; she wasn't aware that you'd be the one she would end up marrying, but it's clear by her lack of surprise that she knew something. At least enough to get her to play along when she should."

"This is messed up," I muttered in disgust as the office building came into view. My grandfather would be waiting for me and if he heard I was fighting against our bargain, then shit would hit the fan. "Fine, I'll play along but I'm not going to be in charge of the wedding. Hire a planner and get her to report to the girl; let her sort it out."

"That's going against the contract," Silas replied with a huff of amusement. I shot him a look of annoyance.

"I don't fucking care."

My grandfather stood with his back to the door when I walked into my office, waiting just like I knew he would be. Silas and Kai took one look at him and left before he could turn around, their footsteps silent.

"Has the arrangement been finalized?" Grandfather murmured before facing me, cold eyes scanning me for weaknesses that I knew better than to give him.

My jaw clenched before I answered him, throwing my keys down on my desk as I sat down. "There were a few amendments to be made, but I expect I'll be getting the final signed copy on my desk in the next hour or so. The wedding is in four weeks."

"Congratulations then," he responded in amusement, moving away from the windows to settle across from me. "And have you figured out who's leaking company secrets to our competitors?"

"I'm working toward tightening security protocol at the moment. There won't be another leak."

"There better not be. We lost forty million dollars due to the last one." His answer was cold as he reminded me about the previous deal with Bourgetti. It took me a full three months to get them back on board for our newest software. I was well aware of the consequences after losing their previous deal.

"I'm well aware," I bit out as I fought the urge to run my fingers through my hair.

Grandfather finally relaxed enough to let a small smile play on his lips as he leaned back in the leather seat across from me. His face pulled into a smile that would've been normal on anyone else but settled morbidly around his cold eyes. "Good. So, when can I expect the invitation to your nuptials then?"

"As soon as the wedding planner has gotten started," I answered carefully, cataloging his responses while wondering how much interest he had in my wife. A little was too much at this point. I had to be careful.

"Wedding planner," he murmured, raising an eyebrow. "From my dealings with the Altaha's, the wedding will be your responsibility to sort out."

"A form of goodwill to my new bride," I smiled evenly as I picked up a nearby pen and hoped that was the end of the conversation.

"Hmm," Grandfather answered, watching me keenly as I switched on my laptop and grabbed the nearby papers to go through. "Not a bad idea. Your father should've done the same with his bride, maybe then he wouldn't have had the trouble he did."

I stilled at the mention of the broken agreement, my mind flashing back to Lena Altaha, but I kept my face neutral while my fingers flexed on the pen. "I should get back to work. There's a lot to get sorted before my wife starts working here."

"Alright, alright, I can take a hint," he chuckled dryly as he rose from the chair slowly. It was all a part of the image he wanted others to believe. I knew better. At sixty-seven years old, he was a lot more mobile than the rest of the world realized, but that was all part of the game. "I'll see you for dinner tomorrow evening, correct?"

It wasn't a question, I nodded my head, staring at a page that made no sense as I tracked his footsteps striding out of my office. Once the doors were shut, I threw them to the floor with a snarl, watching the papers falling around slowly.

It was all a game, but I was getting so fucking tired of being another chess piece.

Alisha

Being engaged wasn't what it was cracked up to be. A week after I signed the new contract, my grandmother held a party to celebrate my upcoming nuptials. Talon and I escaped half an hour into it and ended up stealing the liquor in Grandfather's locked office cabinet before we left to get wasted on my couch.

"I can't believe you're getting married before me," he muttered, still in shock.

I had an L-shaped couch in my living room, chosen specifically for days like this. Talon always took the longer end, while I took the chaise part, legs curled to my chest.

"I know," I responded, sipping from the bottle of champagne before I passed it to him. The top of our heads bumped into each other as his arm flailed hopelessly a few times, and I snickered at the sight.

Eventually, he grasped the neck of the champagne bottle and managed to take a sip. "I thought you had a few years to go still," he added.

"I know."

"I mean, who was the youngest to get married? It was Luna, I think, and she was like 26."

"I know," I repeated irritably. Talon opened his mouth to say something else, and I grabbed a pillow to smack him over the head. "I KNOW, OKAY!"

"Ow! Never mind; I was going to feel sorry for you, but now I don't," he replied and as he sat up, he shoved the bottle of champagne my way. I took it and gulped, feeling the liquid burn down my throat and not stopping until the fizz made my eyes tear up. "I wonder what your wedding's going to be like."

His words brought to memory the *thing* that happened this afternoon and I choked. After sputtering on champagne, I shoved the bottle at Talon before he could thump me on my back. "About that..." I cleared my throat before admitting, "My husband-to-be doesn't really seem to care about wedding arrangements."

"It's in the contract, though," Talon gave me a confused look, his eyes red from how many times he'd rubbed them in the last hour. The culprit was my gorgeous white and gray ragdoll who snuggled on his lap. If Tal didn't have such a soft spot for Ora, then he wouldn't be sitting sniffling every time he visited.

"Yeah, I know, but he seems to have found a loophole," I answered, snatching up Ora and cuddling her to my chest. Tal's allergies might not have been severe, but I didn't want him to asphyxiate accidentally because he was stubborn. "He hired a wedding planner. She called me today to let me know and apparently, she's helping me pick out everything for the wedding."

"That's..." Tal stalled, looking for the right word.

"Strange?" I added helpfully and he nodded.

"Yeah, that's strange. None of the others have offered that. Did you speak to Lena about it? I don't want you getting in trouble for something because 'he-who-shall-not-be-named' decided he doesn't want to plan a wedding."

"Yeah, Lena phoned me earlier and she said it's fine as long as I take someone with me. My first appointment with the wedding planner is in a few days. Tal..." I said, carefully gauging his reaction. He glanced back at me with a lifted eyebrow. "Please can you come with me?"

Talon sputtered, then pulled the champagne bottle closer for a sip. "Why on earth do you want me to do that?"

"Because there was one condition," I hesitated then muttered softly. "Avi can't make the first appointment, but because of the contract, someone has to advocate on his behalf until he can be there himself."

"You're kidding," Talon snorted, running a hand through his hair. "Okay, so who'd he ask to go with? His grandfather?"

"His friends."

"Jesus."

I hummed in agreement, pulling the champagne bottle closer for a sip. We were slowly running out of alcohol to go through, which was probably a good thing because the sky was dark outside, and the clock above my mantle told me it was just after midnight.

"Dad wasn't too happy with me during the meeting," I admitted in a hushed whisper. We'd barely spoken about what happened two weeks ago, not because Tal wasn't curious but because I still had trouble dealing with it all. "This contract's a little different than the others. Not that they'll admit it, but I think there was a lot more on the table this time."

"Like what?" Talon asked, and I shrugged, playing with the edges of my crochet blanket.

"I don't know," I sighed.

"Listen to your instincts, Sunshine," Tal murmured in the dark of the room. "Just say the word, and I'll get you out of this."

Relieved, I let out a breath. I knew that's what Talon would've said. There was a reason why Grandfather didn't allow him in on the discussions regarding our marriages, and it wasn't because Tal was still single. Rather, Tal refused to fiddle in other people's lives without due cause. This went against everything he believed in, and that made him the safest person to speak to.

"Love you, Tal," I whispered, nudging his head with my own as he echoed my words.

"Love you, Sunshine."

Chapter 4

Alisha

TWO DAYS LATER, TALON showed up at my apartment with his eyes covered by sunglasses and a baseball cap on his head.

"No," I said as soon as I answered the door. Wagging my finger at him, I stated as clearly as possible. "I don't know what shit you've got yourself into, but I don't want any part of it."

"Great, 'cause neither do I," he replied sarcastically, wincing as he walked into the room. "I'm here to pay my dues as your favorite uncle."

"This better just be about the appointment, Tal," I warned, ignoring him to grab the rest of my stuff. Ora, having heard that her favorite person had arrived, walked into the room and greeted him with a loud *meow*.

"Hey, baby," Talon cooed, bending to pick her up. "Did you miss me?"

I rolled my eyes and checked in the mirror for the third time to make sure I looked as respectable as possible. "I mean it, Tal, you better behave. Don't do anything I wouldn't do."

My dark hair was braided, the thick tail hanging over my shoulder while my bangs threatened to break loose and fall into my eyes. It wasn't the best, but it would have to do. I grabbed a cream coat to wear over the blouse and jeans I'd picked out this morning, double-checking the weather outside where the clouds hung dark and heavy over the city's skyline.

There was definitely rain on the way, if I was lucky then there'd be thunder or hail to accompany it and I'd be able to get out of this appointment without a fuss.

"Yeah, yeah, yeah," he muttered, and a moment later I heard Ora start to purr, indicating he'd either refilled her food bowl (she'd just had breakfast) or she was being carried around. I never understood why she allowed him to carry her all over like that when even on a good day I could barely hold her for more than a hot minute.

"You ready?" Tal called, walking into my bed-room with a sneeze. I hummed in response as he set the cat down on my bed. "I can't believe you're making me come with you to your dress appointment. What am I supposed to do? Hold your purse while you go through the different styles?"

"If that makes you happy," I replied, and he rolled his eyes, mocking my words as we walked out of the apartment and down to the lobby.

"You aren't driving?" Tal questioned under his breath, suddenly serious.

I shook my head in answer and his relaxed countenance faded, replaced by a familiar pro-tective look in his eyes as we walked outside where a car was waiting.

Swallowing down my nerves, I approached the car, unsurprised when someone on the in-side opened the front door. What did surprise me, however, was the sight of those familiar ice-blue eyes that turned to look at me as I climbed into the front seat.

"H—Hi," I stammered, clutching my purse to my stomach. I don't know why I hadn't con-sidered this happening but now that it had, I couldn't quite catch my breath thanks to how fast my heart was beating.

Avi glanced me over, an irritated expression on his face. "You brought a friend with you?"

My mouth opened to respond but Talon beat me to it.

"I'm her emotional support uncle," he dead-panned from the backseat, sticking his arm toward the front for Avi to shake. "I'm guessing that means you must be the fiancé then."

The *fiancé's* eyebrow shot up, but he didn't say anything more than, "Put your seatbelt on," before he steered the car onto the road again.

"You're a real charmer, aren't you?" Talon muttered as I quickly buckled myself in. Avi didn't respond and Talon carried on. "I heard there was supposed to be a wedding planner for these sorts of things. Where are we going and is she meeting us there?"

"Yes," Avi responded shortly before going silent again. I bit my lip, waiting to hear if Talon would say anything but he stayed thankfully silent until we pulled up to a wedding dress boutique, where a woman was standing outside waiting for us.

"Well at least he has some class," Tal informed me as soon as we left the car. Avi had already strode up ahead, so I knew he wouldn't have heard that, but I punched Talon on the arm anyway. "Hey!"

"No, you hey! Stop making things awkward." I glanced over as Avi greeted the woman, and she flashed him a cheerful grin before pulling a tablet out of her bag.

"I'm not making things awkward, iceman over there is." He gestured toward Avi, and I quickly glared at Talon before glancing over. Even with the distance between us, I could see that impervious eyebrow of his raised. "He's rude."

I didn't bother to respond, taking my first step toward the man in question with a metaphorical noose around my neck. It didn't matter how rude he was, I still had to live with him for seven years.

Avi was cold when we met him at the door, but the slight tic in his jaw let me know his patience was running thin. The man was wound up tighter than a spring, and that made me wary. If I'd known he would be coming with then I would've invited Lena instead of Talon. At least she knew better than to piss off my future husband.

Talon, unfortunately, had no apparent survival instinct because as soon as we walked past Avi, he smacked him on the chest and stated cheerfully, "Cheer up! I'm sure whoever pissed in your breakfast is already regretting it by the look on your face."

I stifled a groan before turning toward the auburn-haired woman with a smile, "Lovely to meet you, I'm Alisha."

"I thought so," she teased before holding a hand out. "My name's Court, we spoke on the phone. Thank you again for allowing me to work with you, I promise to do everything in my power to make your wedding a dream come true."

"Thank you," I said, smiling politely as I shook her hand.

"First things first," Court said, motioning toward the building behind her. "Your fiancé let me know that you haven't got a dress picked out just yet. Unfortunately, a lot of places are booked out, but I managed to get you an appointment with Adrianne Spires. She normally has a few original pieces that she gets from designers all over the globe. Vera Wang, Dior, whatever you have your mind on she could probably get for you."

The men stayed silent, and I fidgeted before responding. "Cool."

My lack of enthusiasm took a little bit of Court's sunshine away, and she appeared crestfallen for a moment before gesturing for me to step in front of her. "If you follow me, we can get started and I'll go over a few more appointments lined up while you're trying on a few things."

Talon coughed to cover a laugh, and I shot him a glare before smiling politely again at the wedding planner as we stepped into the boutique.

Inside a woman with a sharp blonde bob came out. "Courtney! Darling, you made it." They hugged, air-kissing for a moment before turning toward me. "And you must be Miss Altaha. I've heard all about your engagement! I don't know how you both kept it secret," she winked, her familiarity coming across as shifty.

"That's right," I answered with a polite smile. I didn't like the way she was eyeing me, and her pointed glances toward Avi only made things worse. My cheeks flushed, the tabloids hadn't caught the story yet, but I had an idea that the news might be out sooner rather than later at this rate.

"Wonderful! My name is Adrianne, I see you've brought guests. You're all just on time. Would you like anything to drink before we go through the options?" No one answered, the air slightly tense, and her smile dimmed slightly before brightening once more. "Alright! Well, if you gentlemen wouldn't mind, my assistant will be in shortly to show you to the waiting rooms. Miss Altaha, if you'll follow me?"

With butterflies in my stomach, I shot Talon one last warning glance and then followed Adrianne and Court through to the dressing rooms.

Avi

It wasn't my intention to attend a dress appointment, but someone from the Altaha's side had given my grandfather a call and *persuaded* him to make me come along. Whatever was said had pissed him off properly because he'd phoned me right after to let me know.

Kai and Silas didn't seem too surprised when I let them know about the change of plans, but with the girl's *emotional support uncle* here I was already reconsidering letting them off the hook.

I recognized Talon Altaha at first glance, but I never realized he'd be a pain in my ass the second he got into my car. I doubt he recognized me though. At 27 years old, he probably didn't remember applying to intern at my company eight years ago, but I had difficulty forgetting after the trouble it caused me when I declined his application.

Whether the Altaha's knew it or not, they'd had a hand in every decision I'd made over the past twenty-something years. All thanks to this contract. I should've paid more attention to getting out of it when I was younger, maybe then I wouldn't be sitting waiting for Alisha to come out of the dressing room in one of the many white dresses hanging around.

Thankfully, Talon grew bored of his own bullshit half an hour ago and was busy scrolling through his phone while we waited.

"Tal?" Alisha's called as a door opened, her doe eyes peaking at me first before she finally glanced at her uncle. "Can you come here a sec?"

"Oh, Cher, don't be shy," the dressmaker laughed, and I gritted my teeth in annoyance when she ignored Alisha's sputtering and pushed the girl out in front of us. "See, you look gorgeous darling. Look at their faces."

I shot an annoyed glance at the stylist, but despite her words, she wasn't even looking to

see what our expressions were saying otherwise she would've noticed the glare on Talon's
face as well.

Maybe I should get another dressmaker.

The wedding planner shot a worried glance
my way before taking notes on her tablet.

"Right," Alisha muttered, looking uncomfortable as she played with the material
bunching around her hips. I saw her bite her
lip for a second before suddenly a mask came
over her features, the smile almost appearing
genuine except for the fact that it didn't reach
her eyes.

I grimaced at the sight, looking away from
her. "It looks like shit. Try on another." Four
faces gaped at me, and my eyebrow rose.
"Well, we don't have all day. Are you going to
put another one on or not?"

"Dude!" Talon bit out, but Alisha shot him a
warning look and he stilled, jaw clenched.

"I'd like to try on another, please," she said,
turning toward the dressmaker with a whisper. I could've been persuaded to think her
feelings were hurt but the fire in her eyes
proved otherwise and I bit back a smirk when
her voice turned frosty and she bit out, "My
fiancé doesn't like it."

The glare she sent my way only amused me further.

She left, material flaring out behind her, and strode toward the dressing room only to return in a new dress. Alisha tilted her chin up, her eyebrow raised in my direction. I didn't have to wait long to hear the snarl in her voice.

"Well, does this one suit your tastes?" she asked sarcastically, and I bit back a smile. It didn't; in fact, the dress was worse than the other simply because it showed off her curves a little better, but the way her shoulders curved confidentially told me that while it might not have suited my tastes, it certainly suited hers.

Her expression only grew more irritated at my lack of response, and I leaned back into the couch, pretending to be bored. Amber eyes flared and heat lit inside me.

"This is a Vivienne Westwood Vaida from the 2024 designer collection," the dressmaker declared reverently. Her fingers trailed over the silken fabric lovingly. "It's only a test option in the store. It's made to order. If you'd like to go with this option, then we'll have to contact the designer with your measurements."

A wicked smile lit up Alisha's face, "Really? I'll take it."

The she-devil had an expression on her face that could've dropped a lesser man on his knees. Then something happened and her eyes widened before dropping to the floor. "That is, if it suits your taste, Avi?"

I grunted an acknowledgment, annoyed that she sheathed her claws. I preferred the honesty to the saccharine sweet smile gracing her lips when she declared that she'd made her decision.

The wedding planner chirped happily, and the three women left to go through a few more things in the boutique.

I pulled out my phone to hide my interest in the girl but seeing her simper like everyone else irritated me. I didn't bother to question it.

Alisha

After the first appointment with the wedding planner, Avi ended up attending every single appointment after that too. Eventually, I stopped feeling surprised when I found him waiting in the car outside for me. I stopped feeling nervous as well and instead, irritation started to bubble each time he made a rude remark that would cause the people around us to glance at me with pity.

It became harder and harder to control my temper and I found myself grinding my teeth each time, but I never forgot myself like I did at the first appointment. Reminders of my aunt's scars were enough to keep me quiet.

On the second appointment, we ended up going to a cake tasting which led me to the painful realization that my future husband was a picky eater and horrible at disguising it.

"That's awful," he stated after one taste of a vanilla cake with lemon filling. I managed to keep my composure, but then he picked up a napkin and spat the red velvet into it.

Irritation flickered to life and my eye started to twitch. A painful hour later and I didn't bother tasting the cakes that I might like, knowing he would have something shitty to say. He ended up choosing a chocolate cake with raspberry filling. I would've gone for the cheesecake, but instead of letting him know, I painted on a smile as he dropped me off at home again. His tone was irritated when he bid me goodbye, and I was left with a frown on my face when I entered my apartment.

The next appointment was regarding the venue. Of course, if I'd known that then I wouldn't have shown up in high heels. We ended up visiting fifteen different places. Churches, gardens, parks, and different venues in different places, and with each I grew more and more annoyed, quickly excusing myself to go to the bathroom before I said something to jeopardize the contract. Avi had a lot to say, and the wedding planner wilted with each note she made.

After I came back out, it was decided that the wedding would be held at a grandiose church by an apple orchard out of town. My nose wrinkled but I kept myself silent, eyeing my husband-to-be whenever he wasn't looking. Avi dropped me off and a day later I caught a break when the wedding planner phoned to let me know that he couldn't attend due to scheduling issues with a meeting.

"Oh," I muttered with fake concern. "Does that mean the appointment's been canceled?"

"No?" the wedding planner seemed confused when she answered. I didn't really care to explain the dynamics of my relationship with Avi so when she explained that we were going to go ahead, and I just needed to meet her at the next location, then I let her know I'd be able to meet her after lunch. When the time came, I got into my once more black car and ended up at a flower shop to choose my bouquet.

Without Avi there to make comments, I settled on a dark red rose bouquet and left it at that. The appointment didn't even last half an hour and the following two appointments went similarly, but if I thought I'd gotten away without having to deal with Avi then I was dead wrong.

At the last appointment, I walked into a restaurant that was meant to cater for the wedding and stopped in my tracks when I found those sharp blue eyes watching me.

"You're late," he stated, waving off the wedding planner in the corner.

My eyebrow raised and I lifted my chin. "Am I?" Regret filled me the moment I snapped that out. A week of dealing with Avi Zohran and already I was slipping up. I had to be more careful.

Much to my confusion, amusement glittered within the depths of his blue eyes, and he gestured toward the seat across from him. "The appointment was supposed to be twenty minutes ago. We've been waiting for you to arrive before starting."

His words surprised me, and I approached the table with cautious footsteps. "I'm sorry," I murmured, tipping my chin down as I pulled out the chair and sat. "I had an emergency at the shelter."

It wasn't a lie. Just before I'd left, one of my on-site therapists had called to let me know that a woman had given birth in the communal bathroom. We'd managed to get her an ambulance ride to the next hospital, but the cost was severe, and that wasn't including the hospital bills that were still to come. The baby had turned out to be premature, likely due to stress. Before I left, we had been informed by her doctor that she'd be spending the next month and a bit in the NICU. Our finances were going to take a knock, and that only put further into perspective how much I needed this wedding to go on without any problems.

"Was it sorted out?" Avi asked, and I blinked out of my thoughts as a waiter came through with the first set of dishes.

"It will be," I answered, peering through my eyelashes to see a strange expression on Avi's face. It wasn't one I could decipher, not with how little I knew him, and even so, it disappeared a moment later as we started to taste the different dishes in front of us.

"This is nice," he mentioned casually, surprising me again and when I turned to look at him, he was pointing at a spicy crab salad.

"It's alright," I mentioned, considering him carefully. He glanced up at me in contemplation then shocked me into stillness when he asked which I liked. After a moment of silence, I pointed out the vegetable spring rolls. "I'm a fan of Asian food."

Before I could question the look on his face further, Court came out with a brilliant smile on her face. "How's the happy couple doing? We've got some lovely dishes for you to try, but I first wanted to check if you've chosen a starter."

"Yes, we have," Avi answered her with an easy smile. "The crab salad and the spring rolls."

I blinked slowly, seeing Court's shoulders relax as she clapped her hands happily. "Perfect! We'll send out the mains soon," she winked at us, whispering theatrically. "I have it on good authority that we have an amazing, orange-basted ribeye."

The rest of the appointment went smoothly and by the end, Court confirmed everything we'd decided over the past week and promised to make our wedding, "A dream come true!"

I didn't tell her that her words were ambitious, but I did say thank you when I left the appointment and got back into my car to drive home.

Avi

The sooner the wedding approached, the more issues started to pop up at the office. I shouldn't have been irritated about the interruptions; they were a helpful reminder of my priorities. It was fun annoying my fiancé, but the plan had been to break the contract before the wedding, and with each week that passed, it started to seem less and less likely.

"Silas, I can't marry her," I stated simply, fingers in my hair as we discussed it again. It was getting late, and there were a hundred other things that should've been taking my time. Yet instead of discussing the security threats we were currently facing, the newest leak that happened yesterday, or the fact that my contact at a local news agency let me know my wedding would be the hot topic for the next month, I was pacing my office while Silas and Kai staring at copies of the contract in front of them.

"I don't know what you want me to do, Avi, there isn't any way that I can find a way out of this," Silas repeated, and I could tell he was getting frustrated. We all were, but the wedding was going to happen in three days, and I still didn't have a way out of that fucking contract.

"This can't be happening to me right now," I muttered, joining them on the couch so that I could look over the contract again. It didn't matter how little legal knowledge I had, urgency was running through my veins as things started to feel less like a game and more like I would actually be tying my life to a woman in the next few days.

I read through the contract, slipping off my tie and throwing it on the floor as I flicked through the pages one by one. Nothing stood out. Nothing drew my attention. It was just like Silas had said, the contract was concrete which meant unless I broke the agreement I had with my grandfather, I was well and truly fucked.

Muttering a curse, I threw the papers at the table and slumped into the couch.

"Will it really be that bad?" Si muttered beside me. I closed my eyes and huffed out a laugh. They didn't know how bad it would get.

"We can arrange protection for her," Kai responded and when I glanced over at him, his gaze was distant as he considered the details.

"You know it's not that easy," I reminded him, sitting up to glance at the contract again. "We shouldn't even be thinking about what to do afterward. This wedding can't happen. I need to find a way out of it before we get married."

"We aren't going to find the answer in three days," Silas snapped, pulling himself to his feet. "I vote we enlist help."

"Are you insane?" Kai cried out, for once the reasonable one out of us three. "Who are you planning to enlist that will know what to do? You'd have to explain everything to them, and even then, we'd end up going over the same things. It's a waste of resources and time."

"Maybe it is, maybe it isn't. Who knows, sometimes it takes a keener eye to see something we've missed." Si shrugged, his shoes squeaking as he walked the length of my office to grab the decanter of whiskey sitting on a table at the back. With it in his hand, he grabbed three tumblers and made his way back to me. "Otherwise, the next best thing is to marry the girl and hope to god that you don't get her pregnant before you divorce her."

"No divorce allowed within six years," I reminded him, and he snapped his fingers at me with a corrected, "Seven."

Rolling my eyes, I amended my statement and followed it up with, "Not that that matters because we don't have seven years."

"No but what's stopping you from divorcing her afterward?" Kai asked, an eyebrow raised in my direction. "We can continue with the plan, and you can stick it out. She doesn't have to be involved at all."

"That's not possible," I disagreed, not even bothering to think about it.

"It's not impossible," Si said in agreement with Kai's statement. He held out a tumbler filled with whiskey in my direction, and I took it, swallowing the burning liquid as he continued. "Your arrangement with the girl won't impact what you're busy with unless you plan to involve her in anything. Which we all know isn't going to happen. So, make up your mind, Zohran. Are you going to marry the girl or are we going to continue wasting valuable resources to find a solution while you run away from the problem?

You know as well as we do that there are more important things to focus on."

Alisha

My wedding day crept closer and closer, disrupting every part of my life as I considered the changes that would happen in just a few days. Everything in my apartment was already packed except for the furniture and it left me feeling cold and vulnerable each time I stared at it.

Unlike the other women, this apartment wasn't one I'd been renting until my contract took place, it actually was mine. They'd warned me not to buy something frivolous with the little bit of my inheritance that I got at 21 but I hadn't been able to stay at home until I got married. There were too many rules in place, too many things I did wrong, and events I was forced to go to. So, I bought the apartment and then worked damn hard on extra jobs that no one but Lena and Tal knew about to make sure I could keep it.

Every piece of furniture within these walls was earned through my hard work and I didn't want to leave it behind, but I couldn't take it with me where I was going. There wouldn't be a place for it in my husband's house.

I was starting to wonder if I'd fit in there at all.

Ora didn't like the changes, and there'd been multiple cardboard boxes bearing the brunt of her unhappiness when I walked through the place earlier.

"I'm sorry, honey," I whispered from the corner of my apartment. She lay on the couch, her ears pinned back and tail flickering after I scolded her for scratching another box. I knew she was listening, but I hadn't gotten anything further than that after I finished boxing up the last of my things.

I don't know what I'd miss more about this place. Whether it was the memories of getting drunk with Talon on the couch, and mocking the rest of the family, or the skyline that comforted me whenever I was alone. The thought of losing any of it made me sad, and I guess that was the true reason they'd always told me never to buy anything permanent. We always lost it in the end.

My front door creaked open, and I turned my head slightly to see Lena and Talon walking in with pizza and beer that they left on the kitchen counter.

"Sunshine," Tal sang, and Lena rolled her eyes predictably. She was already walking toward my little spot on the balcony.

"Ready for your bachelorette party?" she murmured as she sat down next to me. Her eyes were sad when they met mine, but that didn't stop her from trying to get me to smile when she nudged my shoulder and teased, "Tal's got a bag of vibrators in the car. I didn't tell him though; I want to see his reaction when he finds out."

I started to laugh but the sound came out sounding more like a sob and Lena pulled me in for a hug. "Your life isn't over, little bird," she whispered against my hair. "I promise you, it isn't over."

"How can you say that?" I argued, wiping at my face. "I was supposed to have more time. The others all had years to themselves before they had to change for their husbands. It isn't fair."

"I know, sweetheart, but this deal's been in the making for a lot longer than you think," Lena informed me quietly.

"I don't know what that means," I answered her, sniffing in lungfuls of her favorite perfume until it calmed my heartbeat, and I could repeat my words without hearing my voice shaking. "I don't know what that means."

"Don't lie to yourself, Ali," Lena whispered, and she clutched me tighter against her chest. "I know that you can tell this contract is different. You're smarter than all of us, I know you figured that out already."

I had. I knew it the moment she told me that I'd be getting married years before I was supposed to. Yet that wasn't the question that really bugged me, and it didn't help to ask but I couldn't stop myself from saying something anyway. "Maybe that's true, but it doesn't tell me why it's different. What's so special about Avi Zohran?"

"I can't say," Lena whispered and that left me with a horrible feeling in my gut because the last time there was a contract that was a little more different than the rest was when Lena married her husband and look what happened to her.

Talon returned a moment later, appearing flustered as he dumped a gift bag in front of me. "Why are you two both such assholes? I just want to know, okay? Cause I just had to explain to the valet why there's a bag of dicks in my car and that's not cool."

Chapter 5

Alisha

T HREE DAYS PASSED QUICKLY and before I even knew it, I was walking down the aisle in a dress that felt a little too tight. At least that was the reason I was giving myself when it felt like I couldn't breathe. In reality, the Vivienne Westwood gown was perfectly measured to my body, the silk hugged every curve, yet somehow still managed to glide like water over my skin with every movement.

I loved and hated it. Just like everything else happening today.

My family stood around, gazing in wide-eyed wonder as if this was normal, but I didn't have it in me to pretend. The man standing at the end of the aisle had eyes like chipped ice and a jaw that clenched tighter the closer I got. It sent nerves skittering down my spine like warning signs. There was nothing normal about marrying a person you didn't know.

Contrary to popular belief, my life didn't change the second I slipped my hand into Avi's, and he pulled the sheer lace veil over my dark curls. It also didn't change as we ran through the vows, and then said our customary I do's, but I wouldn't lie and say nothing changed the moment the priest said, "You may now kiss your bride." Because the second Avi's blue eyes focused on me with all of that sharp intensity, my breath disappeared and when he dipped to kiss me, I froze, wondering if those lips would be ice cold when they met mine.

They weren't, and that was even worse.

My eyes fluttered shut the moment his breath brushed against my skin, tasting like mint and oranges and a second later when he kissed me, I nearly lost my balance because Avi Zohran might've looked like an ice sculpture and those eyes might've been sharp enough to cut into a girl, but his lips were warm and soft under mine. And when his mouth opened, I found myself clutching onto his shirt as he gave in and kissed me properly.

Everything changed the moment he kissed me properly.

My whole body lit up like a firecracker and suddenly the world went dead quiet, or maybe I was wrong, and the church actually had gone quiet, but I couldn't really tell because a second later everything was deafening and I backed away on a gasp, my lips tingling from where his had touched him.

I lifted my fingers to touch, feeling shaken, and realized something far more startling than the kiss that we'd just shared.

They were clapping.

I swallowed. The whole church was clapping. God, what was wrong with these people? The only ones who cared that I wasn't a hundred percent after that kiss were Lena and Tal. Not even my parents cared, because from where I was standing it was all too obvious that what Lena had said was true and I could almost picture the dollar signs in my father's eyes as Avi held my left hand up for them to see. Seven years of my freedom and he shares in a security company to add to the Altaha portfolio. It was devastating. That was all we were worth at the end of the day.

I glanced at Avi, my mouth dry after our kiss, and found his face neutral as he faced that fiasco in front of us. I couldn't find anything in his expression to see if he'd felt the things I had when his lips were on mine, and I didn't know if that was for better or worse. I didn't have a chance to question it because I was quickly being tugged behind him as he walked us back down the aisle.

Flowers were thrown over our heads by the occupants attending our wedding and a smile froze on my lips as I walked through the shower of petals. Everyone knew that weddings signified a huge life change, but this was just the smallest one of many.

The details of the contract were clear. I had to deliver an heir to the Zohran name, and not for the first time, I found my body trembling as I realized what that meant. No one really cared about my feelings on the matter, and that terrified me more than the thought of going to bed with a man like Avi Zohran.

The rest of the wedding passed in a blur, but Avi didn't leave my side, smiling charmingly at everyone who came up to congratulate us. It was awkward, and I was too scared to leave my seat in case Talon and Lena would bombard me in the bathrooms. I couldn't explain to them what happened earlier. I still didn't understand it myself.

My wandering thoughts stopped the moment a stranger stepped up to the table, wearing a dark suit with a burgundy tie. He held a jewelry box in hand, the flat square kind that carried necklaces, and placed it in front of me, grinning with a thin-lipped smile that was far too sharp to seem friendly, "A gift for the newest addition to our family."

"Thank you," I murmured, watching the man carefully as I opened the jewelry box. It wasn't the first gift I'd received today. Countless others were going to be transported to my new house when the wedding was over. Yet something about this slim box gave me pause and I fiddled with the cover, almost scared to open it.

My shoulders jolted when the man cried out, "Ah, where are our manners? Introduce me to your wife, my boy."

The demand made my husband stiffen and I glanced at him, taking note of their similarities. That sharp nose and angled jaw were only the smallest details, it was really the eyes that gave it all away. I'd thought my husband's eyes were terrifying, but they were only cold, whereas the stranger's eyes were more than chipped ice, they were cold and empty. Dead almost.

"Alisha," Avi said in that smooth timbre, "Allow me to introduce my grandfather, Heinrich Zohran."

"A pleasure," I uttered, holding my hand out in greeting. There was a smile on my lips, but I don't think it was enough to cover the tremble in my fingers when Heinrich grasped them and laid a soft kiss on my skin. The look in his eyes made me stiffen and I fought not to pull my hand away too soon.

"No, I do believe the pleasure is all mine," he grinned, and I hid my shudder as my lips formed a smile to cover my unease. I slowly pulled my hand away and discretely tried to wipe it on my wedding gown. The sharpness of those cold eyes took me in as Avi's grandfather tilted his head, "Apologies that I missed the main event. However, I hope you both have a very long and happy marriage."

The words were pure sentiment that was clear, and I kept that polite smile on my lips.

"Thank you," I murmured demurely, and I kept quiet as he turned to speak to Avi about a family dinner night. The small talk didn't last long, and he left us to join the rest of the party.

The silence felt weighted, and soon, the necklace box in my hand stole my attention. With a quick glance over at my new husband, I started to open it. Inside was an antique choker in burnished silver. The design was Navajo, with crescent moons, stars, and wolves running against a forest. It was stunning. The moon and stars were made of diamonds, but the wolves were turquoise.

"You should wear it," Avi murmured as he leaned back in his seat to play with the cuffs of his sleeves. "It will match the earrings and bracelets that you have on."

I swallowed, feeling a lump in my throat. The earrings and bracelets that he mentioned were more than what they seemed. Each turquoise and silver bracelet on my wrist had been made by the women in my family. Amongst the blues was one made of amber. Tal made that one and gave it to me the other night while we were lying on my couch eating pizza. *For good luck*, he'd said, but I knew it was more than that. This was him showing his support while the rest of the men in our family abandoned me for their greed.

I don't know what made me do it, perhaps loneliness or sheer stupidity, but I turned to my new husband, and with a shaking smile, I asked, "Would you help me put it on?"

I regretted it the moment I saw the sneer curl his lips.

"Turn around and lift your hair," he answered and the annoyance in his tone was the final straw that shook me to the core. I bit back the tears that came unbidden as he gently took the choker, and I pulled up my hair. His fingers were warm against the skin of my neck and my cheeks heated under his gaze. So much for that kiss. I should've known better than to hope that meant anything.

Avi and I didn't say another word until everything was over, but my trembling increased the moment we walked outside the wedding, passing through another shower of dried flower petals to get to the SUV waiting for us outside. He glanced at me when he opened the backdoor and tipped his head. "Get in."

I stepped up and entered the car, barely looking into his eyes as I glanced around the interior of the car and came face to face with his friends, Silas and Kai.

"Congratulations," Silas said in greeting. We hadn't had a chance to talk during the wedding, so I mumbled the customary thanks and avoided Kai's piercing gaze. Avi slid into the seat next to me, and the door shut a moment later. I shifted in my seat, the distance between us odd after being pasted to his side at the dinner table.

It was hard to breathe in a car full of strangers, and a month of attending wedding planning appointments hadn't really given me enough knowledge to know what I'd be living with for the next seven years.

"The drive to the house is going to be an hour," Avi mentioned as I buckled my seatbelt. From the corner of my eye, I saw him pull out a tablet.

"Okay," I answered automatically and swallowed to try and replace the dry feeling in my throat. The wedding, the people, it was all so much. I settled in, still feeling shocked.

Avi Zohran was my husband, and I wasn't sure what that meant.

I couldn't be certain when I fell asleep but waking up was an experience I wouldn't forget. A loud boom ricocheted, and the car swerved, gravity throwing me forward until an arm snaked out and pulled me back again. I gasped, my hands pressed against the seat in front of me.

"Kai! Watch where the hell you're going," Avi barked, his voice loud in my ear and I jumped. My gaze whipped toward him, noticing the irate expression on his face.

"Get lost, Zohran! You know I hate driving up this mountain." Kai complained from the front, and I was still trying to figure out what he meant when Silas snorted.

"Man, if that's the case then stop offering to drive."

Kai's sneer was clear even if I couldn't see it. "You can't complain! You did the same thing yesterday."

Avi's arm was still around my waist, and I cleared my throat, face flaming when his ice-bright eyes turned my way. "Thank you," I croaked as he pulled away, but he ignored me and settled into his seat, so I did the same only to remember what Kai had said.

"Where are we?" I asked, clearing my throat when my voice came out sounding raspy.

Avi glanced at me with an annoyed expression, and I squirmed in the sudden silence.

"Echo Mountain," he answered finally before turning to face the front.

"Wait? Why are we driving up Echo Mountain?" I muttered, staring out at the rocky mountain landscape surrounding us. "There are wildcats out there."

"That's exactly the same thing I said when he bought it," Kai muttered in agreement and I didn't know what was more shocking, what he'd said or that he'd agreed in the first place.

Avi owned Echo Mountain. I snorted, just barely stopping myself from asking if that meant the whole mountain or just a small portion of it. A ridiculous question, but then again, that was probably the least ridiculous thing about this whole trip.

A few minutes later, the car approached a huge metal gate and idled. There we waited until a few security guards strode over. The moment they saw Kai and Silas, they didn't have to check in the back before motioning for the gate to be opened. Yet I still watched in silence as the car drove through bush and rocks to get to a huge loghouse built into the mountain.

"We're here," Silas stated unnecessarily before he got out of the car and came to open my door.

I mumbled a thanks before I unbuckled and joined him outside in the cold air. This time when my trembling started it wasn't just because I was nervous about what would happen when we got inside, but also because the gown I was wearing wasn't enough to keep me warm when the rain soaked through the material.

"Silas, take her inside," Avi commanded, not even looking at me as he pulled his cell phone out of his pocket.

I gaped at him. Talon was right, he was rude. Silas walked toward me, offering his arm and I shook my head. "No, wait!" I turned toward Avi again, my brow furrowed. "What about my things?"

Avi dropped his phone back into his pocket with a sigh. "Your things were delivered earlier today. We don't have much staff on the property, but those who are there have been advised to leave everything until you have a chance to sort it out."

That was reasonable, and I found myself nodding along before a thought occurred to me. "What about my cat?" I asked, turning toward Avi in time to see his icy expression change to confusion.

"Your what?" he frowned, making me worried.

"My cat," I repeated, stressing the words. "She was supposed to be taken through today as well. Is she there?" Avi glanced at me with an eyebrow raised and I glanced at him with irritation. I actually did want to go inside, but I wanted to make sure that Ora was there first, something I realized that I should've asked before, but it slipped my mind during the wedding.

I heard a snigger coming from the direction where I'd last seen Kai standing, but I didn't look over my shoulder to confirm. If he wanted to laugh, then let him laugh. It wasn't going to change the circumstances.

"You brought your cat," Avi said slowly, and I arched an eyebrow at him—didn't he know that? His face twisted with annoyance before he pinched the bridge of his nose between two fingers and muttered something to himself. "Okay, you know what, never mind. Silas, please help her find her cat and get her inside before she gets sick."

He spoke again as if I wasn't even there, and something inside me stung a little at being treated that way. Maybe it was wishful thinking, but I expected a little more after getting married. Not a declaration of love by any means, his cold attitude since the banquet was proof enough that I wouldn't be getting anything like that, but hell, him finding my cat would be a start.

"Come on, if she was brought here with the rest of your stuff then she's probably inside waiting for you," Silas said, amusement on his face and I nodded my head before following him up the steps and into the house.

As soon as we stepped through a large wooden door, Silas and I were greeted by an older woman with a gentle smile on her face. "Rosa," he grinned, bending to kiss her cheek. "Have you been well?"

"Oh, I've been fine, and you know that," she shushed him with a laugh, playfully pushing him aside to approach me. "Goodness! I thought the boys would never bring you back. Now, let me have a look at you. What's your name, sweetheart?"

"Alisha," I answered as my fingers tightened on the fabric of my dress. I didn't feel like an interrogation. I was wet and cold, and I really just wanted to check on my cat to make sure she made it here alright.

Instead, pale brown eyes met mine and the older woman grinned before enveloping me in a hug. "Well, it's lovely to meet you dear. Let's get you up to your room and you can have a nice warm bath to get rid of the chill."

"Thank you, but I just want to know where my cat is first," I replied, stepping out of her hold.

I settled the moment Rosa said, "She's in the room waiting for you. A noisy one that, but very beautiful. I hope you don't mind, but I gave her some warm milk to make up for that horrid travel up the mountain."

"That's fine, thank you," I whispered, closing my eyes in relief.

"No worries, now come. Follow me so that we can get you into something warmer. I'm sure you aren't comfortable in a wet dress." Rosa grinned, directing me up the stairs, and toward a door at the end of the hallway.

I was greeted by a meow as soon as I entered the room, and I let out a breath as Rosa closed the door behind us. Without my worry for Ora, I could finally take in the place that I'd be living for the next seven years. Starting with the bedroom which had a modern, rustic appeal. Like a luxurious log cabin. Floor-to-ceiling windows adorned the far side of the room, and from what I could tell, they were a lot darker than normal. Nearly black, which meant there was some sort of tint to make up for the lack of curtains. That gave the room a modern feel, while everything else made it purely rustic.

The rest of the room was decorated in paneled wood. The furniture, the floors, and even the walls. The floor had a geometric design that must've been terrible to clean, and the wood on the walls was a lot thicker but placed in a herring design. It was gorgeous, and so was the furniture.

In the center of the room was a coffee table, which stood in front of a fireplace with a TV hanging above it. The table was surrounded by a green leather chaise and two similar high-backed chairs. Ora sat on the one, until she saw me enter the room, then with a purr she jumped off and strolled over to me.

"There's a bathroom through that door there," Rosa stated, and she walked past a huge California King and swung open a set of French doors on the left. They opened up to reveal a walk-in closet that somehow led into a bathroom. "Your clothes are all still downstairs at the moment, I'll bring a few up so long and help you pack them into the cupboards. Avi mentioned that you wanted to sort it out, so I didn't want to interfere, but I'm sure he won't mind his wife wearing one of his t-shirts if you'd like to get out of that wedding dress."

Wife.

I blinked at the floor in confusion as Rosa left the room. That was going to take some getting used to.

Chapter 6

Avi

S HE BROUGHT A CAT with her. I scowled as I strode toward the kitchen, pulling my wet jacket off and throwing it on a nearby barstool beside Silas. A fucking *pet*, and no one thought to mention a single thing about that while we were getting the movers to put her boxes all over my house.

"What's the plan now?" he asked, his fork clinging against the warm spaghetti Rosa had dished up for him. There was a whole pot of it on the stove, and I didn't hesitate before getting a plate and dishing a good scoop up. The scent of herbs and her homemade tomato sauce filled the kitchen leaving my mouth watering. Nothing beat her cooking.

"Tomorrow, she starts in the office. We can use her as a distraction, but this isn't a permanent solution. You need to find a way out of this contract before Grandfather figures out the plan," I said, spinning the pasta around my fork until I had enough to bite into. I couldn't eat during the reception, every time someone came up to us, Alisha stiffened. The resulting heartburn was fucking with my concentration.

"You wanted her to be your assistant, does this mean she gets the same clearances as the last one?" Silas moved to place his dish in the sink, pulling his cell phone out of his back pocket to scroll through. "I need to know what I should give her access to, Avi."

"You aren't going to give her access to anything that can implicate us," my tone grew cold. "I don't know her well enough to trust her around that information. We'll give her simple things to work on until we can get a better grip on the security of the company. We'll keep her busy around the office, throw her in with a few departments every week, and make her take on a few menial tasks. It's just to keep her out of my house until this whole charade is over."

His brow furrowed in thought. "You think she'll find evidence in the house?"

I shrugged. "Anything's possible. It's a risk I can't take right now."

We stood silent for a moment, both lost in our thoughts as the rain started to pitter-patter again outside. Eventually, Kai joined us in the kitchen, his face serious. "I just got a phone call. The lab's been broken into again."

Fuck, not now. My eyes squeezed shut and I snapped out irritably, "How the fuck does this keep happening, Adakai? Our systems are the best there is, how the hell is someone getting through things? What are we missing? Who was working there tonight?"

His jaw ticked, but Kai was good under pressure. There wasn't another sign that he wasn't happy about this news. "I'm finding out now. I've sent the security team their orders, they'll get back to us within the hour."

"That isn't good enough, get the keys, we need to check up on this ourselves."

"If I may," Silas interrupted as I turned to place the bowl in the kitchen sink, I raised my eyebrow and waited for him to finish speaking. "You just got married. If you want to placate your grandfather, then you need to play along. That means you can't rush to the office at nearly ten at night to find out what's going on. It will be better if Kai and I go investigate."

"I'm not going to stay and play house when the company is crashing under my watch. My grandfather would understand that much given the circumstances." I scrubbed my jaw with a growl.

"He's right," Kai said, his eyes hard. "If we know anything then the old man will demand an answer the moment, you're in the office tomorrow. However, in saying that, you can't show just up in the same suit you got married in. Imagine how that will look tomorrow when you show up with your new wife?"

"Wasn't planning to. You guys have clothes here." They both did, it made it easier on nights when we needed more time to brainstorm without letting my grandfather know what was going on.

"What, you're going to leave your fancy suits for a pair of jeans?" Kai snorted, ignoring my glare. What I wasn't going to do was walk upstairs where Alisha was currently waiting. If that meant wearing their clothes, then so be it.

Several hours later, we were at the lab where half the security team and all our night shift staff were waiting.

It was quiet after they'd given their reports and now everyone was sitting around waiting for the verdict. This shouldn't have been so fucking routine and it pissed me off more that everyone was so casual about going through the processes. We were on a schedule now, looking for indications of the break-in but there wasn't any broken glass to step onto, the windows and doors were all intact, and there was no damage besides the fact that my multi-million-dollar microchip had been taken right from under our noses. Whoever decided to rob us clearly knew what they were doing. My suspect list remained the same, we had no answers. There was no one I hadn't already checked. I scratched at my jaw.

"Are we certain that this is everyone who was working here tonight?" I motioned toward the group of people standing nearby.

Maya nodded, her face weary from working so many hours. I made a note to amend the shift schedule, knowing she wouldn't be happy with me for doing that. "Yes. This is everyone. We were working on the advancements mentioned in yesterday's meeting before we realized someone else was in the building."

That was the official report. Someone broke into the offices intending to steal the latest microchip while Maya and her team had been working on the changes I requested. Changes that would've allowed the technology to understand its own energy flow and adjust as needed so that the medical team could get as much out of it as possible. Those were the changes I'd requested because at the end of the day, we were hoping to encourage governments to buy the technology not just private purchasers and yet that meant fuck all if someone had just stolen the updated microchips.

Questions ran rampant in my mind as I considered it all. How the hell had they known the tech would be completed today? We hadn't even had much of a deadline until my grandfather strode into the room two days ago and demanded he wanted to see the latest results. He wasn't happy. He never was so we had the meeting and staff were given double the compensation to work through the night to finish with the microchip before our meeting with the board of directors next week.

That information wasn't public, another sign pointing toward it being someone within the company. Yet the staff had all been searched already, and so were the guards before we checked every single security feed. Somehow, in the midst of all of this, after the alarms had sounded said person had managed to run out of the building without being caught by any of the many cameras or even the security detail we had working here non-stop.

Nothing made sense anymore. How the hell had my life gone from the one plan we had been working on to trying to figure out who was planning to sabotage us and avoid a woman I married without actually intending to get married?

"Kai, Silas, my office now." I strode out of the room and toward my office on the penthouse floor. My mind was spinning, nothing about this shit made any sense.

Four break-ins. Information was stolen right from under my nose and given to several of our competitors. *Given* being the operative word. We had already figured out that it was the same person breaking in each time, but the information kept being spilled to different companies to keep us off their track.

"We need to move offices," I said as soon as the doors were closed behind us, heading toward the bar. "This can't keep happening. The microchip's gone, yet the alarm was triggered and no one on the security team was able to catch anyone running out. It just doesn't make sense."

"Are we still thinking it's foul play?" Kai asked as I poured three tumblers of whiskey. I grabbed mine and with a groan, I tipped my head back toward the ceiling. There was a tension headache starting in the base of my neck.

"We've suspected foul play from the beginning," I answered, searching for answers on the gleaming white surface. Mine was the only office where there weren't any cameras blinking with a red light. The only place safe enough to speak in. "No one came in and no one has left. That means that someone inside there right now is guilty."

"All of our staff have been thoroughly vetted," Silas replied with a confused expression. "Anyone planning on taking information that they don't own will be sitting with one hell of a lawsuit. Why would they risk it?"

"I don't fucking know, man. Money? Fame?" I shrugged with a scowl. "Look, none of that matters at the moment. Once we catch the person involved then we can sort out the motive. For now, we need to get a handle on the situation. We need a new place. Rent or buy, I don't care. I'll sign the papers tomorrow. We need to sort out security and staffing immediately. I want each team to be shifted with our private security in the lab at the same time. Any signs of foul play need to be brought to my attention and the suspects dealt with accordingly." *Speaking of shifts.* "Also, we need to get Maya to cool it for a bit. The last thing I need is my head engineer burning out before we even finish with the design."

"Yeah, I saw that too." Kai paused with his glass halfway to his lips as he considered it. "I'll check in with her shifts to see how many hours she's been pulling. Maybe we can get her more assistance."

"No." I shook my head. "I don't want anyone else working on this project until we can find out who is leaking information and stealing from the company. Until then, we'll slow down and give everyone a chance to figure out what's going on. We're still the only person to come up with this sort of technology. We have some time before the rest figure out how we're creating it."

"What are we going to do about the staff at the moment?" Silas questioned as he poured himself another few fingers of whiskey. "We've kept them for five hours, Avi. We need to let them go home or we're going to be sitting with more problems than just missing information."

I knew what he meant. We didn't want to deal with labor lawsuits at the moment with everyone present.

"Next plan of action?" I muttered, more for myself than the others. There were so many plans and yet we were getting nowhere. My fingers delved into my hair as I considered it all.

"We need to divide the teams to try and find out how often this happens," Kai replied casually as if it would be so easy to split up the over two hundred employees working on this project. Never mind the thousand-plus employees working for the company. "We need to cross-reference everyone."

I slammed my hand on the table with a curse. "How the fuck are we going to go through so many employees to find out which might be the cause of all this shit?"

"No one here has time to go over that all," Silas confirmed but something about his tone drew my attention and once he saw he had it he continued. "Alisha is starting tomorrow. I've read her file; the girl is smart. She has a double major in Business and Finance and enough credits to get her master's if she ever feels like it."

"It could work," I spoke as I stared at my glass. It could even keep her busy instead of questioning the parts of our agreement that I didn't want her to know about.

Alisha

My sleep was interrupted the moment he opened the door to the bedroom, and my heart nearly stopped right in my chest at the sound of his clothes hitting the floor. Now? I knew that most people had sex on their wedding night, but this was one thing that was never discussed in my house.

The arrangement was to get us married to wealthy families and after that, we were on our own. What happened afterward was up to us.

Seven years was a long time to be married to someone you hated, but what if I didn't have a choice? What then? Would I have to learn the hard way just like my aunt? Or would they save me before it got too bad? The questions were never-ending, yet there was no one here to listen and even fewer people who could answer them.

Just a few feet away, I heard the unmistakable sound of shoes hitting the floor and then suddenly the bear of a man who was my husband fell onto the middle of the bed and right on top of Ora who let out a yowl as she squirmed out from under him and onto me, puffed up and hissing at his frozen figure.

He didn't yell. Not like I expected him to. Nor did he curse. In fact, for a few minutes, the room was so silent that I could still hear the bats squeaking as they flew past the window.

"The cat's in my room," he said, and I was so startled I couldn't even think what to say to respond to that. Where did he think she would be? We weren't in the city anymore. I couldn't let her walk around when something bigger and scarier could pick her up for dinner.

Swallowing past my dry throat, I croaked out, "Well where did you expect me to put her."

A loud sigh answered me. Long and drawn out. For a man who signed a marriage contract, he didn't sound very excited to hear I was waiting for him. I didn't know what to do with that information. Then again, I didn't really know what to do with a husband either.

What would he want from me? According to Rosa, Avi Zohran had people who cooked and cleaned for him, but he didn't like many other people in his house, and in some areas only she could go in. Like his office and bedroom. One which I'd been warned Avi wouldn't be happy if I entered and the other, she'd opened up for me and even managed to get my cat settled in. Or as settled as Ora was going to get considering Avi nearly squished her just a moment ago.

He didn't break the silence to say anything else, but rather got up from the bed and walked toward the bathroom without a backward glance. And in the dim light that shone through a moment later, my cheeks flushed as I realized he'd all but stripped to his underpants before getting into bed.

Despite what he'd said, I couldn't fall back to sleep after realizing that so instead I drew myself up into a sitting position with my back to the headboard. That's where I stayed, with Ora pulled to my chest to calm her down after her fright. Her fur was still puffed up and she made little disgruntled noises as I rubbed her down.

At least twenty minutes passed before Avi returned to the room. I met his gaze silently as he glanced my way, but it wasn't long before he left, fully dressed once more. I let out a breath, not sure if my relief was due to the sudden emptiness after his presence had departed or if it was because he'd come into the room in the first place.

"Dear god, Ora, what am I going to do here?" I whispered when the door closed after him. She grumbled and I let her go, falling onto the pillow that smelled faintly of mint and oranges with a hint of spice that I couldn't figure out.

I couldn't fall asleep after that encounter, and I stayed up the rest of the night waiting for dawn to break. Eventually, it did, the gold and pink sun splitting through the bedroom and across the bed.

His clothes were still on the floor when I got up, and my cheeks heated once more when I realized that there was a pair of boxers in his jeans. Was he naked when his body was pressed against my leg?

Chapter 7

Alisha

K NOCKING ON THE DOOR interrupted me while I put my boots on. Thinking it was Rosa, I finished zipping them up before calling out. "You can come in."

Avi stepped into the room, and the surprise made me blink. "Were you knocking?" I blurted out, noticing the dark circles under his ice-chipped eyes.

He cleared his throat, skin turning red for a moment. "You could've been dressing."

"Right," I answered, still confused. I always hated thinking of myself as property but the way my parents had given me up so easily yesterday still left me with a stinging in my chest. They looked at me like I was another chess piece to trade for more business, just like the rest of the women in my family, and I guess there was a part of me that expected Avi to view me the same way.

Silence followed my answer, and I stood up from the bed before walking toward the mirror. Rosa and I had managed to put a good portion of my things away for me which I was grateful for. It helped me find things this morning to get dressed like my makeup, toiletries, and clothes to wear even though I had no idea how the day would go today.

"I wanted to find out if you would like anything to eat before we go to the office." Avi's voice was closer than I thought, and I spun around to see him glancing down where his clothes had been thrown last night. My cheeks heated as I answered the question he hadn't voiced.

"Your clothes are in the laundry basket in the bathroom."

His eyes turned glacial, and he bit out. "I didn't ask you to do that."

"I wasn't going to leave them on the floor," I muttered.

Avi let out a breath, his brow furrowed as he looked around the room. My things were all over the place, something that made me feel uncomfortable, but Rosa insisted. She even hung up the three-foot dreamcatcher I had above the bed. It was another gift from Talon and Lena, from when I was younger and used to have nightmares. The feathers were snowy white, and the leather was dyed a pale green to match the jade wolves hanging on to it.

I saw the moment when Avi's eyes locked onto it, but he didn't give it more than a cursory glance before walking out of the room, his gruff voice calling out over his shoulder. "Foods in the kitchen if you're hungry. Be quick, we're leaving in ten."

My eyes narrowed, and I sighed, glancing in the mirror once more before walking out wearing a black woolen skirt and boots with a silken violet blouse.

"Don't be late," I mocked. The jewelry I wore at my wedding had been placed into a small drawer that Rosa showed me yesterday, everything except for Talon and Lena's bracelets which were still on my wrists. I would need their strength today of all days.

Walking toward the kitchen, I grimaced at the sight of my things piling up everywhere. Avi's house was big, but it was still a lot smaller than the places the rest of my family had. It was also a lot bigger than my two-bedroom apartment. According to Rosa, there were five spacious rooms, each with its own bathroom, the kitchen, the living room, his home office, the dining room, and the rest I hadn't had the chance to explore yet. She'd given me a tour after the men left, telling me about her schedule and the people who worked here.

The cleaning staff came in twice a week, on Mondays and Fridays, but she was the only one who came in three times a week, the added Wednesday was when she normally ran through a few chores and then did most of the grocery shopping. She offered to get me things when she went this week, but I didn't know what to say to that. I didn't know what I would need, or what would be allowed without it being too much of a problem. Until I had an idea then I would buy my own things. It was better that way.

The only thing I didn't know was who would be in charge of cooking while Rosa wasn't here. According to her, Avi and his friends often ordered pizza or cooked for themselves. This brought me to another question: *Why were they living in the house with him?*

It was strange, but too many strange things were happening at the moment, and I could only fixate on one thing at a time. Like my first day at work. *His* work.

I walked into the quiet kitchen and glanced around with my bottom lip between my teeth. When Avi said there was food, he didn't really mention that I would have to make it myself. I blew out a breath of frustration and walked toward the fridge for an idea of what there was. Fresh vegetables, milk, cheese... There was yogurt inside but being that I was lactose intolerant that would make life a nightmare, so I left the fridge and turned toward the cupboards. Cereal, dried fruit, canned food, and dry cooking ingredients were stored in the pantry. Atop the microwave were eggs... Avi had said ten minutes, and I was slowly running out of time. I made a note to wake up earlier tomorrow morning and grabbed a small handful of dried fruit to eat on the way.

A car's hooting hurried me along, and I grumbled under my breath, tempted to slow my walk just to piss him off.

By the time I left the house with my purse slung over my shoulder, the dried fruit was done, and Avi had one of his SUVs idling in the driveway. I hurried over quickly and got into the front seat with an apology on the tip of my tongue until he opened his mouth.

"You need to be quicker; I can't wait forever for you to get your stuff ready," he muttered before steering us both away from the house.

The apology disappeared as annoyance buried deep under my skin. The way he said that made me feel like a child getting scolded. I kept my mouth shut and put my seatbelt on before he commented on that too, then settled in for the longest hour of my life. It wasn't the first time I'd gone hungry before.

I shouldn't have been surprised that the grump didn't even listen to music on his way to work. He struck me as a man who didn't know what fun was, and for a moment I entertained the idea of letting him know exactly what type of person I was. The idea made me smile but it dropped when I realized that I couldn't do that.

Avi wasn't like Talon; he probably wouldn't appreciate my sarcasm or the music I listened to and the last thing I wanted was to make an enemy out of someone I had to live with for the next seven years.

An hour later we pulled into an underground parking, and I don't know why I was so surprised by the security measures that they had in place. The underground parking had security outside checking the staff and their vehicles before letting people through while on the inside there was a security detail on every floor. Uniformed men stopped each staff member but let Avi and me through without any hassle.

Their faces were professionally blank, but I didn't miss the flicker of curiosity when they saw me at their boss's side. Avi didn't say anything the entire way and my legs were burning to keep up with his quick stride.

Zohran Tech was nothing like the small, two-story building that Chrysalis occupied downtown. It was professional. Corporate. Nothing like the homely little charity that I built from the ground up but everything like the businesses that my family had. It had a similar modern design as the hotels, with silver and white marble floors and art on the walls. There were potted plants in every room, simple ferns in black, square ceramic pots stood in various places on the floor, standing as tall as my shoulders. Glass vases stood on every table with a mixture of flowers to brighten up the space, and the furniture was sleek and expensive.

There had to be hundreds of staff walking around but surprisingly none of them were in uniform. I don't know why I was expecting them to wear similar clothes, like robots, but instead, everyone wore business casual and the space around me felt a little friendlier for it.

I let out a breath of relief the moment I realized we were walking toward the elevator, and I didn't miss the twitch of his mouth when the doors closed. When they opened again, we were on the top floor of the building, and I walked into a room that was far more comfortable than the floors below. It was spacy and bright, in part because of the design and also because the left side of the room had floor-to-ceiling windows covered by blinds which were opened slightly to let natural light into the room.

On the far side of the room was an empty reception desk with a turned-off computer and on either side were doors leading to two more offices. On my right was another two doors. It was clear that this was some sort of waiting area.

Dark brown leather couches stood around a coffee table, almost similar to the arrangement in Avi's bedroom. They were decorated with plain jade green cushions, and a framed painting of a meadow of lilies was on the wall above them. A massive cream rug was on the floor and my feet were nearly silent as I padded after Avi.

Kai met us by the doorway of one of the offices, a black mug in his hand and tired eyes that brightened when a mischievous smirk took over his features.

"Good morning Mr. and Mrs. Zohran," he greeted, the tone teasing. Avi gave him a flat glance in response and turned toward me.

"Silas will be up here soon to help you settle in. There's a coffee machine in my office if you want to grab something to drink," he stated, pushing past his friend to get through to what must have been his office.

I followed behind quietly, passing mahogany bookshelves with large books and bronze decorations. Simple things that were purely there for design and nothing else.

His office mirrored the one I just left, with the same wooden furniture and green accents. A beautiful mahogany desk stood near the wall of windows, filled with papers and his laptop while in the middle of the room, the floor dipped to include a leather L-shaped couch like in my apartment at home and a coffee table. It was more informal than I would've thought, and I eyed it all in consideration, stilling when I noticed the bar.

That's different.

It took up a good portion of space, but the office was big anyway. Behind it was a shelf of different glasses, coffee mugs, and other things. Water bottles, snacks. The sort of things you would see in an apartment and not an office. It made me wonder how much time my husband spent here that he felt the need to add all of that.

Avi settled in the leather chair behind his desk, not bothering to glance my way, and I frowned momentarily, feeling awkward as I watched Kai walk toward the bar and sit on one of the taller bar stools, setting his coffee beside another laptop. What did they want me to do now that I was here?

The bag that I brought with me doubled as a laptop carrier as well as a handbag, so if there wasn't anything to do then I could run through my emails in the meantime. Still, I didn't want to presume.

I glanced over at Avi; it was clear that he was already consumed in his work. There was a furrow between his eyebrows and a determined set to his jaw as he flicked through the papers on his desk. I bit my lip for a moment, wondering how he could make anything out of that mess, but the sound of a coffee machine stole my attention, and I glanced over at Kai in question. Didn't he have coffee when we walked in?

Kai met my gaze, an expression of amusement on his face as he gestured toward the couch in the middle of the room. "Have a seat, I promise we won't bite."

I met his wary gaze, feeling doubtful but I walked toward the preferred seat anyway, glancing back at Avi once more before I sat down. Ice-bright eyes stole my attention, and my cheeks flushed at his slow perusal before he turned that sharp gaze to Kai. "If you're making coffee, grab me a water too please."

"Do I look like your assistant?" Kai snarked in reply, but he still pulled a bottle of water from the shelf and tucked it into his back pocket.

"Well, I'm not going to make it," I muttered to myself, my face turned down to avoid them seeing the scowl I wore. A snort let me know they must have heard me anyway, and I froze. Thankfully, that's when Silas walked into the room, a beautiful blonde a step behind him.

"Morning everyone," he greeted, his eyes twinkling when they met mine.

I muttered a greeting in response while Kai saluted the pair and took a sip from the black coffee mug.

"Maya, Silas," Avi tipped his head before going back to his work.

The blonder woman, Maya let out a yawn as she crossed the distance toward the couches, her hand held out for me to shake. "Hi, I'm Maya," she said, and I shook her hand with a smile, wondering what I should say.

"Maya, this is Alisha, Avi's new wife," Silas introduced, shooting me a warm smile before explaining. "Maya's going to help us get you all settled in. Has Avi explained any of the duties you'll be taking on?"

I shook my head in answer and saw his eyes shift toward Avi momentarily, not that he would get any answer out of him. Avi didn't seem to care about speaking, his focus was on the paperwork in front of him. Even so, I swear I felt his eyes on my back as Maya mentioned she would show me how to use the coffee machine.

I followed her to the bar as Silas settled in on the couch, opening a laptop on the coffee table in front of him.

"You'll mainly be helping us out with paperwork and scheduling meetings," Silas spoke from the couch as I grabbed two black cups from the shelf behind us. The cups hung from my grasp as I flicked my eyes in his direction, and my lower lip caught between my teeth. I had two degrees and they wanted me to do paperwork? Silas carried on as he typed a few things into his keyboards. "Due to recent security measures we've had to let go of our assistants and that's made us get a little behind in paperwork."

He seemed to feel my gaze on him because he flashed a smile my way. "Don't worry, you'll also be helping Maya out with a few things."

"Maya is my head engineer," Avi stated from the other side of the room, and I glanced at him in time to see him flash her a warm grin. It bespoke familiarity and my heart felt like a piece of ice in my chest, pumping cold through my veins. It was nothing like the smirks that he'd given me this past month.

"We've all had to adjust to keep our work as quiet as possible, and it's causing a strain."

His eyes turned to me, cold as ice and calm as he surveyed my tense frame. I softened my posture and adopted a relaxed demeanor, but something told me that he didn't buy it, his eyes sharp even from so far away. "Silas and Kai run separate firms belonging to Zohran Tech. We have multiple subsidiary companies that all work alongside Zohran Tech to provide the support needed in the work we do. You'll find out more from them as you help them out. Any questions?"

I shook my head in a no as Maya took the mugs from my hands and placed them on the tray for the coffee machine. In the silence of the room, she hummed to herself as she popped two capsules in and pressed a few buttons to get the machine going. It whirred to life and dark liquid poured into each mug.

"Maya," Avi called, glancing over after we each had our mugs of coffee. His eyes didn't look my way this time and I shifted on my feet. "Kai, Silas, and I need the office for a meeting. Please take Alisha on a tour of the buildings and make sure that she's put on the system. You know our hours. I don't want to have any difficulties because some idiot forgets who she is."

Maya nodded her head, stifling another yawn as she pressed her palm over her mouth. "You got it, boss," she muttered before flashing me a tired grin. "Come on, it's nice to have another girl to chat with."

I followed her out quietly, pulling my bag over my shoulder as I spared Avi one last glance. I always knew it would be weird, but this was turning out a lot worse than I thought it would.

Thankfully, the morning wasn't as bad as it could've been, and Maya turned out to be a lot more fun than I would've thought at first glance. She was bubbly and outgoing, always turning toward me with a grin. She showed me around the building, and it took a lot longer than I thought. I couldn't tell if that was on purpose or not but at least it gave me the chance to familiarize myself with the building.

We visited an office on the third floor first and Maya went straight to the Human Resources department to get me an ID card.

"You'll probably have access to about them as much as I do if you're helping out," she shrugged as we left, but her chatter wasn't enough for me to avoid the staff that eyed me every time I walked by. Maya caught my frown and nudged me with her shoulder. "Don't worry about them. You're Alisha Zohran now, so it's going to take some getting used to. Even with that though, I doubt Avi and the boys will have you working with the rest of the staff. I think you're just going to be helping us out with a few things."

"Because of the security problems," I murmured, reminded once more about the things that Lena told me a month ago. Zohran Tech was having difficulties with information being leaked.

Maya's face looked more exhausted than before. "Yep. We're all running around like headless chickens to try and figure out how the information is being leaked. We can't afford to have all that work stolen."

"I'm sure that's a lot of stress," I answered carefully, the last thing I needed was for them to find out about Lena's digging.

"It is. Avi's been working really hard to get this project off the ground," Maya's voice warmed at the mention of his name, pulling me from my thoughts. I glanced at her and found her eyes distant, and her smile tinged with sadness. Why would she look sad about that? I would've thought that she'd be happy to talk about her project considering she was the head engineer for it. Unless... my mind flashed back to the warm grin on Avi's face this morning. I could see then that they were just familiar with each other, but I honestly thought it was more friendly than anything. Was I wrong about that?

It stopped me in my tracks, and she took a few steps before looking back at me.

"Is everything alright?"

"Yes, sorry, I was worried I would spill," I smiled apologetically, holding my coffee cup up for her inspection. There wasn't that much in it to spill so easily but thankfully Maya looked too tired to question it, and I followed her down the hallway, listening to her carefully as she showed me the rest of the company.

My mind started turning around the idea as Maya showed me the cafeteria on the first floor, and the security division on the second floor and then just walked me through each of the floors, explaining who worked there and what they did. She seemed to know everyone in the building and while they greeted her with the same friendliness as she showed me, it was clear that there was a professional boundary in place. It made sense, after all, she was technically in a senior position.

I followed along without a problem, taking note of my surroundings and the different departments but I couldn't help thinking about the warmth in Maya's tone whenever she spoke about Avi, and she spoke about him and the other guys a lot. There was warmth in her voice when she spoke about Kai and Silas too, but something told me there was more between Maya and Avi than the others.

"Have you known them a while?" I asked casually as we walked back into the waiting room on the top floor. Avi's door was closed, a possible indication that he was still in a meeting with Kai and Silas. I turned my attention back to Maya and found her shrugging.

"We were friends as kids," she explained which made sense if I thought about it. Her grin was infectious as she teased, "I could tell you so many things about them."

"You should," I said with a laugh just as Avi's door opened and he walked his grandfather out. I shifted on my feet at the sight of Heinrich, feeling that same slimy feeling that I'd felt at the wedding.

"Alisha!" he greeted cheerfully, his eyes flickering toward Maya and me. I expected her to greet him warmly. After all, if she had known Avi, Kai, and Silas since they were young then theoretically speaking, she should've known Avi's grandfather too.

Strangely though, I watched Maya's smile die out as Heinrich patted his grandson on the shoulder, a gesture that should've seemed normal but looked uncomfortable from where I stood.

"Enjoying your first day at the office, girlie?" Heinrich questioned, the smile on his face still sharklike. Did Maya's discomfort mean that I wasn't the only one put off by Heinrich's keen eyes?

Glancing over at Avi, I tried on a smile that hopefully appeared a lot more cheerful than it seemed. "Yes, thank you, sir. Maya has been amazing in showing me the different floors." What was it about Heinrich Zohran that made my stomach roll?

"Yes, Maya would know the place well," he commented, and I could've sworn that I felt Maya's body tense. Strange.

"If you don't mind, Grandfather, but I'd like to get Alicia settled in. There's a lot of paperwork that we need sorted," Avi cut in, his eyes as piercing as the man beside him. Yet when they met mine, heat coiled low in my belly instead of the feeling that I got when Heinrich grinned.

Annoyance flashed across the older Zohran's face, but he peered at the watch on his left hand and hummed to himself. "That's quite alright. I have to get going anyway, there's a meeting that I need to attend this afternoon with the board."

I kept my face neutral at his words despite the confusion they instilled. Why would he be attending meetings when Avi's the CEO? Was Lena wrong in her investigation? I thought Heinrich stepped down.

"I should go to," Maya blurted out. "Would you like me to walk you out, sir?" She peered at Heinrich, and he smiled gratefully at her.

"That would be lovely, thanks, dear. Before I leave though," Heinrich turned toward Avi with an apologetic glance. "I wanted to mention that family dinner. I'm afraid that I'm going to have to postpone for a while. I've been invited to join a cruise for a few weeks in Florida, but we can continue again after that. My sincerest apologies, Alisha, I was looking forward to getting to know you." He turned to me with that last bit, and I just barely stopped the shiver at the coldness in his eyes.

"That's alright, thank you," I answered lamely, my coffee mug held awkwardly as Heinrich nodded and walked out, Maya one step behind him.

"Alisha?" Avi's smooth voice cut into my thoughts, and I turned toward him, blinking at his expectant glance. He tipped his head, an eyebrow lifted arrogantly. "Paperwork."

Right.

Chapter 8

Alisha

M Y FIRST DAY AT Zohran Tech ended up being completely normal for an assistant. Avi and I barely spoke to each other while Silas showed me the paperwork he wanted done while I was in the office. I didn't have a problem with that, Silas was friendly, and he explained the things he wanted in a way that I understood without any problem. What I did have a problem with was that I was stuck doing admin instead of running my business. Any of these men could've done the same paperwork in just as little time as it took me.

The rest of the day passed by quickly, and I drove home with Avi on another silent car ride. I'd ended up missing lunch as well, and my stomach was clenching painfully by the time we got home, aided by the awkwardness in the car. Thankfully, Rosa had a meal cooked and ready when we came in through the door and both Kai and Silas joined us for dinner. It eased things, probably because they kept up their friendly banter, but it was still awkward. I didn't fit in there and none of the men knew what to do with me either.

After dinner, I walked toward the bedroom feeling an inkling of dread. It was Avi's room, just because my cat and my things were there didn't make it mine. My fear turned out to be unwarranted though because Avi didn't come through at any point of the night and I only saw him the next morning when he knocked on the door again. His eyes didn't meet mine when I opened the door, and I heard Ora meow from the couches.

"Silas made breakfast," he muttered, still not looking at me. He ran his fingers through his hair, still wearing yesterday's office clothes and I wondered idly if he slept at all the night before. The dark rings under his eyes said no. "If you're happy with it, I'd like for you to come with me again today just to get more familiar with things."

I didn't mind, and it made sense when I thought about it, but my mind was still stuck on him knocking. Was he going to do that every morning? And if he was, did that mean that he wasn't sleeping in his room anymore? A hundred more questions ran through my mind, all of them to do with why Avi would marry a girl like me if he didn't actually want to be married in the first place.

"Why do you keep knocking?" I blurted out again. His eyes met mine then as I was staring, and I felt a flush rise to my cheeks as they traced a path down my figure. He didn't have to say anything, I got it. I shouldn't be judging how he looked, no doubt I didn't look any better in my pajama shirt and shirts.

Avi didn't answer, brushing past me and walking toward the bathroom. My mouth dried up when he unbuttoned the shirt, dropping it to the floor. His muscles flexed in the dim light of the bedroom and for a minute; I felt jealous that the light hadn't been on the night before.

In the dim light of the bedroom, I could see everything I missed the night of our wedding, and I bit my lip at the sight. I'd always been a sucker for the athletes and while Avi didn't seem like a man who played sport, it was clear he worked out. The muscles in his back were proof of that, and the heat pooling between my legs was shocking. So were the thoughts of running my palms up his back and toward his tense shoulders.

He didn't glance back, and I scampered out of the room, my face flaming when the shower started.

Kai and Silas were already out of the kitchen when I walked down, but there was a plate with an omelet waiting on the table for me and I ate it, making myself coffee while I waited to hear the telltale sign of Avi leaving the bedroom. Then I rushed back up the stairs to get dressed for the day, not meeting his eyes when I brushed past him.

An hour later, I was sitting in the office and working through the paperwork that Silas left for me to do. He wasn't even in today, but I'd seen Kai ambling outside the door. He came in every now and then for a coffee, which was odd because I was almost certain his and Silas' offices were right on this floor as well. The last door had proven to be the bathroom which was optimal because then we didn't have to rush down to a lower floor when the elevator took its time.

Maya walked in grinning cheerfully, "Hey, boss man, mind if I steal your assistant?" There was a glint in her eye that made me curious, and Avi muttered something under his breath, waving his hand for us to go ahead.

"Come on, Alisha, we better run before he changes his mind," she winked and this time I couldn't stop the smile from forming as I grabbed my phone and got up from the couch to join her.

"Gosh, is he grumpy today or is that just me?" Maya said with a deadpan expression, and I stopped in my footsteps to glance at Avi.

Ice-bright eyes were narrowed on us. "I'm not in the mood, Maya."

"You're never in *the mood* for anything," she called over her shoulder, not even glancing back. It was clear that she didn't expect him to do or say anything in retribution, but I wasn't so certain. The Avi that I'd met during the appointments was notorious for throwing a tantrum. I glanced at Avi warily and his eyes flicked from Maya to me. An eyebrow raised before he turned back to his work. He used to at least comment now and then, but since the wedding, he'd been quiet. Grumpy, like Maya said.

I bit my lip, frustrated. Were things really going to be this awkward between him and me? I couldn't survive seven years like this. Letting out a breath, I moved toward the doorway until his lazy voice froze me in my place.

"She's taking you down to the cafeteria. They don't charge so you don't need to take your wallet. You didn't eat lunch yesterday, make sure that you do today. I'd prefer not having to phone your father or your grandfather because you collapsed in my office."

My heart skipped a beat and I turned to face those ice-bright eyes once more. I didn't even realize he had noticed that but maybe things wouldn't be as bad as I thought.

"Would you like me to bring you something?" I offered, my hand on the doorknob. It was a truce if he was clever enough to realize that.

A smile ghosted his lips, something genuine but then it was gone again. "Maya knows what I like."

What did he mean by that?

I left the room, my mind spinning but not enough that I couldn't smile when Maya hooked her arm in mine. "Come on, those boys are go-

ing to drive you stir-crazy with their silly paperwork."

My laughter rang out before I could stop it.
"Yeah, it is painful, isn't it?"

Her eyes were sparkling and the grin on her
face was almost familiar. "I know the absolute
best way to get back at them for that."

Something shifted and I felt an easiness that
hadn't been there since the day I got married.
"Really? You have to share then," I grinned.

We reached the cafe in record time, and I
scanned the menus while Maya went straight
up to the girl at the front. "Hi Ash, could we
please get three slices of chocolate cake, a carrot cake slice, two tacos, your pepperoni pizza,
three sandwiches, and..." she paused, glancing
around, and then grinned when she spotted me
gaping. "Whatever, Mrs. Zohran is having."

The girl behind the counter sputtered, staring at me with wide eyes and I stuttered an
order for the cheese croissant for her to ring
it all up. My face flamed at the attention, but it
didn't last as long as I thought, and Maya and
I ended up sitting at a nearby table while we
waited for our order.

"I live for the carrot cake that they have here,"
she declared happily, glancing over at the cake

waiting under a glass dome. Her face was utterly serious when she faced me, but her words weren't. "I'm telling you, if I had to choose one thing to survive on for the rest of my life then it's gonna be that cake."

I chuckled, "Same, but with waffles."

Her eyes lit up and she swung her hand up. "Yes, queen! High five."

I high-fived her and we both snickered before falling into silence.

Twisting my new wedding ring around my finger, I glanced up at Maya. "So how did you become friends with Silas, Kai, and Avi?"

"Silas is my brother," she stated and when my eyebrows rose, she nodded. "I know right? I can't see it either, he's disgusting but the birth certificate doesn't lie. Anyway, he, Kai, and Avi all went to school together. We spent summers at each other's houses, and eventually all ended up working here after college."

"You've known him for a while then," I muttered, wondering if I could trust Maya to let me know what I should expect from my new husband. It was a strange thing to ask, and I didn't even know if she was aware of the circumstances of our marriage but at the end of the day, it wasn't like I could go to anyone else in the family for advice.

"Yeah, I have," she said softly, reaching over to squeeze my hand. "I can't imagine how scary it must be." Her voice wasn't loud enough for anyone to hear but I still grimaced.

"It's a family tradition," I shrugged. There wasn't anything more to say than that.

Maya's eyes still shone with sympathy. "Even so. I wouldn't know how to act in your shoes. You're very brave for not letting it get to you. Avi's a good man, Alisha. You don't have to worry about him."

Those words shouldn't have meant that much, it wasn't like I knew Maya enough to trust her, but they eased a part of my soul anyway and I let out a breath before we switched to small talk. It was nice, I'd never had a girlfriend before that wasn't family.

When our orders arrived in brown paper bags, Maya moaned in delight, clapping her hands excitedly. "I can't wait to have that carrot cake. I've been wanting a piece since last night."

I chuckled to myself, following her back up to the top floor again where it turned out that Avi, Silas, and Kai were all waiting for us.

"Is that food?" Silas called out, his hair sticking up in a million directions, but his eyes had the same sparkle as Maya's.

"Like, totally!" Maya cried out, bypassing him completely. "But Alisha gets first because you suckers made me go fetch it all."

The guys groaned, even Avi surprisingly, but Kai was the first one to rise from the couch and grab a brown bag. Maya passed me my little brown box with the croissant in it and I smiled in thanks before opening it up and taking a bite, watching the others as I ate.

Kai unpacked everything onto the table, grabbing three boxes for himself and retreating to his seat again. Silas was next, and Avi last. I had to hide my grin when I realized that the chocolate cake was for the guys. Who knew they had a sweet tooth?

Things became easier once we settled into a routine. Avi woke me up every morning so that he could come shower and drove me to work on the days that I had with him. For a little while, I wondered where he was sleeping but that question was answered on one of the days that I stayed at the house. I ended up having to work from home that day. I'd been trying to find a pen when I stumbled on Avi's home office and found the stack of bedding on the couch.

Guilt swamped me at the sight, and I wondered if it was because of how freaked out I'd been the night he brought me home with him.

I left the office, making a plan to mention sleeping arrangements with him. There had to be another way around it.

Thankfully, that night Kai and Silas ended up working late so when Avi walked in the door, I confronted him.

"Are you sleeping in your office?"

His face blanched and he took a step back, but that could've been because I was holding a wooden spoon up near his face. I whipped it behind my back and mumbled an apology. "Sorry. That's not—Never mind." I blew out a breath of air and glanced at him again. He looked shell-shocked; it was almost amusing.

"Where are you sleeping?" I tried again, my tone softer.

"Why does it matter?" he asked, wiping his feet on the mat at the front door. I watched him take off his jacket and hang it up, trying to explain. It was hard. Two weeks had gone by, and we'd barely been speaking.

"Because," I swallowed, deciding to go with honesty. "It's not fair for you to sleep on a small couch in the office when I'm taking your bed."

"You and the cat," Avi corrected with amusement, walking toward the kitchen. I followed him, smelling the stew I'd decided to make after seeing the rain outside.

"Me and the cat," I echoed.

"Alright," Avi nodded, eyeing the food on the stove with interest as he turned to face me. This was probably our most civil conversation aside from him threatening me to eat lunch during the day, I smiled with amusement, but it faded the second he raised his eyebrow in question. No way was I going to explain that.

"All I'm saying is that if you don't have anywhere to sleep then it's only fair for me to either sleep on the couch or in another room." I scratched my cheek, then realized I still had the wooden spoon with me. With a frown, I placed it on the counter.

"I'm not going to make you sleep on the couch," he slanted a look my way. There was a smirk on his mouth as he said that, and I shifted on my feet. Was he suggesting what I thought he was suggesting?

"You can't sleep naked!" I blurted out, then smacked a palm over my mouth with a curse. Avi chuckled, the sound heating my insides. "That's not what I meant."

"You didn't mean that I can sleep in my room, but I need to have clothes on?" he raised an eyebrow.

"Yes— No, wait. I did mean that." I glanced away, swearing under my breath. "If you're comfortable, then you can come to sleep in the room with me but not naked. I'm not comfortable with that yet."

God, I had to be the only person in the world debating this shit with my husband. Did my sisters need to do the same? I scowled at the ceiling, if they had then no one told me about it.

Avi stepped close and I swallowed, my focus on him as he tugged a piece of my hair and then reached for a mug from the cupboard. "Fine, we can try that."

Avi

This was the worst idea ever. Alisha was wide awake next to me, obviously thinking on the same line of thought yet neither of us said anything and I wondered if this was actually my job to sort out. After all, I'd agreed to this stupid plan because my back was aching like a bitch this morning. Clearly, that wasn't a good enough reason because a stiff back had nothing on a stiff dick.

My pillow smelled like her, and it was actually pathetic that I was growing a boner of the scent of daisies on my pillow but after two weeks on the couch, I clearly didn't realize that things could get worse.

Alisha sighed and the duvet shifted as she pulled it over her shoulders. The cat was purring somewhere nearby, and I nearly shat myself when she jumped on me half an hour ago.

I reached down to adjust my boxers, laying on my side with a grimace. Then she started snoring.

Guess I was wrong about us both thinking this was a terrible idea. I whispered a curse, shifting again. It wasn't that her snoring was loud; it was actually really kind of cute, but the problem was the fact that she was sleeping right next to me while I was wide awake and staring at the wall.

Grumbling again, I tried to turn over in a way that wouldn't knock into the pillow tower she piled up next to me. Good god, I had been myself for thinking it was funny at the time because now it just seemed sad. My wife had pillows stacked up to avoid us touching as if I was going to do something she wouldn't want. I snorted. Not on the agenda.

"Are you going to keep moving?" her voice reached me, it sounded tired and annoyed. Wasn't like she was dealing with blue balls at this time of the night.

"I can't sleep with the pillows next to me," I muttered in defense. It wasn't a lie; I needed more space to settle down.

A slim arm reached out and tugged the pillows away. "There! Now quit it!" she hissed, turning to face the opposite side again.

I smirked, but it wasn't funny the next morning when I had to sneak out without letting her know she'd been pressing against my wood for most of the night.

Chapter 9

Avi

I DON'T KNOW WHY I thought that Alisha working with me was a good idea. There was no avoiding her. The point had been to keep a close eye on her until I could serve her the divorce papers for this sham of a marriage, but I didn't take into consideration how much she would end up invading my space. All it took was one glance at her in her sleep shorts and I grew hard.

Every. Single. Morning.

We'd been sharing the bed for two weeks, and I'd been forced to wake up earlier and earlier to avoid her realizing she had her ass tucked up right against my hard dick. I don't know how she didn't realize it and I really didn't know why I kept punishing myself like this. I could've kicked

Kai and Silas out, or at least moved my clothes to another room in this house. And if that didn't work then I had to find a way to get out of the house. Maybe get Rosa to clean one of the hunting cabins, and sort it out with proper furniture so that I could use it until this was over.

Despite my arguing, I wasn't blind. Every move she made drew my gaze, but I couldn't do this when it took riling her up to see her snap at me. It was impossible not to and it was so damn easy too.

Three days a week, she came with me to the office and no matter how much I tried to explain that we needed an assistant, it was clear that Alisha was overqualified. And she fucking knew it too. After the first week, it didn't take her long to catch onto the work and soon it was only a few hours, and she was done with everything. Yet I couldn't send her back to the house where she could find evidence of the shit I had against my grandfather.

Silas, Kai, and Maya had their own work to do. Chasing around someone in the company wasn't easy and we were still trying to work through the employees to figure out who was spilling the information. That meant that for three days a week, Alisha would finish her work and then start getting bored. I couldn't fucking take it when she was bored.

It started with her heels tapping, slow, calculated. After ten minutes, she inevitably would start pacing but it was subtle. Moving shit around by the bar and then working her way toward my table. I watched her out of the corner of my eye, every day, waiting to see when she would make a comment. Inevitably, she did.

She would make small remarks about the state of the papers, a system that might've seemed chaotic to her but made sense whenever I worked through it. My new wife was clever, I'd give her that.

"Do you want me to put anything into a binder?" she would ask, pointer finger tapping her lip as she considered the table. Or "Would you like me to file any of those away?". It was the same question changed up each time. She grew braver, less subtle, and eventually just started organizing my table when I went to the bathroom.

Like now.

"Alisha," I spoke calmly, staring at the desk in front of me. The agreement for the new office was gone, and so was everything else that I was working on.

"Yes, Avi?" she answered sweetly, that saccharine smile readily in place. I eyed her warily; after living in close quarters for two weeks, it didn't take a genius to know that she was up to something.

I couldn't move her to the reception table in the front because then I would need an excuse when I moved her back in a few weeks. How the fuck did I explain to her that I didn't want her where my grandfather and his buddies could see her? Kai and Silas knew about the reasons, and they didn't blink twice when Maya and Alisha worked at the bar or near the coffee table. It was better this way. Safer.

It was also harder.

"Where are my papers?"

"Hmm?" she answered absently, fiddling with the coffee machine. Always fucking fiddling. I was starting to think she did it on purpose just to irritate me. Seems like something Maya would've told her. They'd become friends really quickly.

"Where are my papers?" I repeated the question, turning around slowly until I could see her properly.

"Where they should be," she answered, blinking at me calmly. My eyebrow raised and I glanced back at the desk where they should've been. "*Oh!* You mean those papers."

"There aren't any other papers that I would be referring to," I replied flatly as she pulled a black mug from the coffee machine tray and sipped at it slowly.

I waited as she walked toward me, her gait a slow saunter that she seemed to do just to piss me off. The little shit was getting cheeky.

"Do you mean the confidential documents that were lying on your desk?" she asked, tilting her head to stare at the same empty table that I'd been staring at for five minutes.

"Were there any other papers on my desk?" I asked wryly. As a CEO, the documents were always confidential—Company reports, payrolls, and financial reports. It was always the same. Alisha knew that. After doing the paperwork in the office she knew that *very* well. I didn't keep my other documents here. That was just asking to get myself in shit.

"Nope." She popped a biscuit in her mouth and turned toward the couch, ignoring my narrowed eyes as I followed behind her.

"I need the agreement for the new rental," I said as calmly as possible, swallowing hard when she bent to place her coffee on the coffee table.

"It's in the rental files, Avi," she answered before pulling out her laptop. There were two on the table that she worked through depending on the workload. I didn't mind her doing the charity work here; the whole assistant thing was just to keep an eye on her.

I could've stopped then and just gone to the file to fetch the fucking contract, but I didn't want to do that. Alisha wasn't the only one getting bored. I'd been staring at fucking financial reports all morning because the project had slowed down.

"Can you *fetch* them?" I asked, an eyebrow raised. It was dangerous, riling her up like this but fuck, the sight of her when she glared at me made me feel like I was high.

I needed to get laid.

Can't do that either, I reminded myself, sinking my hands into the pockets of my slacks as I met those amber eyes. The marriage contract was like a noose around my neck.

"You can't?" Alisha replied, one eyebrow raised and a dry look on her face.

"Nope," I echoed her earlier response, my blood heating up the second her lips pursed,

SIENNA ADAMS

and she looked me up and down. It didn't take much more than that normally, but instead of that huffed growl she got after I annoyed her enough, today she smiled sweetly and placed her laptop beside her.

My eyes narrowed as I watched her rise from the couch and walk toward the shelf, pulling out a black folder. What was she planning?

A moment later, I had the contract in my hands and no excuse to continue annoying her. That bothered me more than it should.

"Alisha?" I called, walking toward my clean desk. I shouldn't have carried on, but after two weeks of walking around with blue balls, it was easier to piss her off than it was to sleep with her.

"Avi?" she mimicked, slowly closing her laptop.

"Coffee," I demanded, a smirk working its way onto my mouth at the sudden silence behind me.

"Coffee, *what*?" she answered a second later, her voice frosty.

"Coffee, *please*," I rolled my eyes, setting the contract on the table. "And while you're at it, can you get me those financial reports that you packed away?"

Looking at them again was the last thing I wanted to do, but it was better than watching my wife when she started to shuffle around, reorganizing my office.

The silence should've made me realize that I'd gone too far, but I didn't question it, still smirking as I watched her place her laptop down and then move toward the kitchen to make the coffee that I asked for.

A second later, I regretted that when she walked straight up to me and slammed the coffee cup on my desk, spilling half of it onto the floor.

"I am *not* your assistant," she hissed, her eyes narrowed like I was waiting for.

Alisha

"Technically, you are," he drawled in response, and I had to grit my teeth before I said something I shouldn't.

There are a lot of things in life that I will regret but after working as an admin for Avi and his friends, I was finding it difficult to regret splashing his desk and pants with the coffee that he demanded.

Ice-bright eyes glared at me as I turned to leave but we'd been together a month and by now, I should've known that Avi didn't let something go so easily. He got up from his desk, walking a step behind me as I headed to the couch but then I stopped, confused. I glanced down at the hand he'd placed on my wrist and then flicked my eyes toward his icy expression.

"You spilled, spitfire," he murmured, voice as hard as the tension in his face. Was he really that angry for a bit of coffee on his pants? I blinked at him slowly, an eyebrow raised in challenge. Despite all of that, his fingers on my wrist were so gentle.

"Did I?" I questioned but my voice came out more breathless than I would've liked.

"You're going to have to clean it up," he stated, pulling me closer.

"You need help cleaning yourself up?" I challenged, trying to pull my hand away. His grip firmed, stopping my attempt and I could feel my heart racing in my chest.

A devilish grin curled his lips, "Did you think I meant me, spitfire?" That smirk stayed as he traced his eyes over my figure. "I meant my desk. Go grab some paper towels."

He let go of me then and walked back to his seat, but I felt his eyes on me as he sat down again and my whole body trembled as I went to fetch some of the paper towels that were by the coffee machine. I nearly dropped them when I turned around and found him leaning back in his seat, his gaze hungry and that smirk still in place. His eyebrow raised and I hurried up, feeling heat on my cheeks.

I realized the problem when I set the first paper towels down on the desk and then bent to clean up the mess that spilled on the floor. Avi had a big desk, but he made sure to roll the chair away just enough that when I bent to wipe the floor, my body brushed against his legs.

The tremble in me increased as I placed the paper towels down, but it was the clenching between my legs that made it harder for me to stand up again.

"Did you think you'd get away with that?" his voice rolled over me, smooth as caramel and when I turned to face him, I had to grab onto something for balance. The problem was, the thing I grabbed onto wasn't the desk. It was Avi's thigh.

My mouth dried up as I met his gaze, and Avi leaned forward to cup the back of my neck. "Answer me, spitfire." I nearly whimpered at the growl in his voice.

"Yes," I admitted, feeling foolish. This wasn't my first attempt at annoying Avi. The man didn't give me any space in the house, every morning I had to rush out of the room because if I didn't then he started undressing right in front of me!

"Really?" he mocked, fingers soft against my neck. He leaned down lips parted to say something and my own parted in response as I remembered what it felt like kissing him. It was a month ago, but after sleeping in the same bed, I'd been expecting him to snap a lot sooner. We both ignored the fact that he was hard every morning but that didn't mean I wasn't wet when he left. Heat banked in my stomach now just like it did then, and I whimpered at the same time as the door opened.

"Avi?" Maya called, walking right up to the desk. I squeezed my eyes shut, praying she didn't see me there, but the effort was futile cause I heard the moment she did. "I've got the update on the— Oh."

Yeah. Oh.

"I'm going to leave these outside," she stated, her voice wavering as guilt swamped me.

I knew it, my mind whispered as I heard her stride out of the room. She was in love with him, and here I was on my knees between his legs. I had a horrible feeling that I just lost all chances of becoming Maya's friend.

Avi

I couldn't look at Alisha after dropping her off at the house. Maya's face when she spotted us had brought me back to reality and the moment that she left, Alisha jumped up and ran to her spot on the couch without another word. I was left to clean up the mess on my desk, which if I was entirely honest, wouldn't have been there if I hadn't fucked around to begin with.

I sent Rosa a text that afternoon to get a hunting cabin ready. That's it. The last thing I needed was to fuck my wife when I had divorce papers waiting.

However, clearly, I was the only one who thought that because Maya sent me a text message after running from the office to giggle in her lab.

Maya [12:32]: Told you so! :)

Her message wasn't what bothered me though, it was the fact that she told Kai and Silas about what she saw as well, and they started messaging me as well.

Kai [14:35]: That was quick. Hope you used protection otherwise grandaddy Zohran's gonna get that heir he wants so badly.

Silas [15:12]: My sister's blowing up my fucking phone. Please tell me she didn't actually walk in on you and Alisha??

Silas [15:12]: Did college not tell you anything about locking a door behind you?

I ignored their messages, not responding until I saw Alisha walking stiffly inside the house.

Avi [18:55]: Recon at the Dancing Gorilla.

The Dancing Gorilla was a bar on the opposite side of town, somewhere my grandfather and his spies had yet to find me and the moment I walked into the doors I spotted the three vultures waiting patiently, different expressions on their faces. Maya looked gleeful, while her brother was tapping his phone on the bar, glancing at her in annoyance. I had no doubts she hadn't been spending the past few hours annoying the shit out of him with questions.

I dropped into the booth, groaning into my hands as Kai chuckled to himself. "Man, you're so fucked, and you haven't even taken this girl on a date yet."

"I thought you were divorcing her?" Maya asked, suddenly serious. "You can't play with her feelings Avi, she's a lot younger than us." She seemed protective over the girl suddenly and I rolled my eyes.

"I am divorcing her," I muttered, signaling the bartender.

"Then sleeping with her is a bad idea," Kai snorted, calling me an idiot under his breath.

"I gathered. I'm moving into one of the hunting cabins until we can sort this out. Silas, how far are we on breaking the arrangement?" I brushed my fingers through my hair, remembering the look in Alisha's eyes when my fingers were drawing circles on the back of her neck.

"I can't find a way out of it and most of my resources are currently focused on getting the information on your grandfather," he mentioned casually, leaning against his sister as he grabbed a fry off her plate.

Alisha

I shouldn't have been upset when the house was empty that night. I told myself that over and over. There was a lot I could do while the house was empty. Like snooping around, or having a quiet night in, but no. I was too busy thinking about the *incident* in the office, and what would've happened if Maya hadn't walked in when she did. To distract myself, I started wondering instead where everyone was... where *he* was. And that wasn't any better.

I assumed that he would've gone back to work, or maybe out with Kai and Silas but the moment I sat down on the couch in his room with my plate of food and a glass of wine, I started wondering if he went after Maya instead. Her voice might have warbled because she was embarrassed but after hearing her gush about Avi so often, it was easier to assume that seeing me like that had made her upset.

Thankfully, the next day was a Tuesday which meant that I wouldn't have to go into Zohran Tech. I finished eating, swallowed the last of my wine, and went to bed but my sleep was restless because I kept waiting to hear Avi or one of the guys walking around outside the room. Instead, the house was quiet with only Ora and I there and I ended up staring at the ceiling for most of the night.

If Avi returned, then I didn't pick up on it and the next morning, I left the house early before he could wake me up, grabbing a smoothie on the way to work.

I hadn't had as much time at Chrysalis because of the *work* that Avi had me doing at Zohran Tech instead. He'd hired me as the assistant after I made a fuss about it during the first week. If he thought I would forget, then he wasn't as smart as I gave him credit for. I wouldn't have been able to keep up with everything and I had almost felt smug when I realized that he would be in charge of paying her salary every month.

The girl I chose was five years younger than me and barely out of high school, but she'd been volunteering at Chrysalis since I started it and deserved the extra income. As good as she was though, there were things that not even she could pull off for the charity; like organizing a Gala.

I'd been thinking about it for a while now and the best way for me to increase the charity's money would be by pulling my grandmother in to help me with a party. She knew enough about the wealthy living around us that I could make a list of the top fifty people who would bring the most financial benefit to the organization.

"Morning!" Alison greeted me cheerfully as I climbed out of my car.

"Morning, Alison," I replied, pulling out a smile just for her. I couldn't let what was going on between Avi and me affect the work that I did, and Alison was especially sensitive to harsher environments. That's one of the reasons I'd chosen her for the job. She knew what it was like coming back from an abusive household and that experience made her more knowledgeable than another girl with a business degree under her belt.

We walked toward the women and children shelter, our steps in sync as Alison debriefed me on everything that had been going on while I was gone. "I made that booking for you and your grandmother today at the steakhouse she likes. That should help persuade her to join the Gala planning. Then we've received word from the hospital that our mother and baby are going to be alright and can come home. I contacted Lena to make payment arrangements and we'll be bringing them home tomorrow. We've already gone shopping for the baby things you asked for and the rest of the girls wanted to find out if it's alright for us to go ahead with a welcome home party?"

"Sure, I'll check and see now this morning how much money we've got and then you guys can go ahead," I agreed easily. That would give the volunteers and the women something to focus on. They needed that every now and then.

"Great!" Alison flashed me a grin, then as we climbed the stairs to my office, she let me know the grocery shopping would need to be done today, and that we had two more women with kids coming in lately.

I listened with half an ear, nodding along when I had to. We didn't work directly at the shelter, but sometimes I liked to pop in to check on things. On the days that I could come through, I would help with the shopping and cleaning, sometimes even the cooking too and today seemed to be one of those days.

Before I left to get lunch with my grandmother, Alison and I went shopping for more food and then spent the morning among the women.

There was a therapist who worked on-site; she and Alison were staying in the house with the women, and they helped me cook an enormous batch of spaghetti for tonight before I left. The girls who stayed here were given breakfast and supper, but we couldn't afford to add lunch to that list just yet. Thankfully, when it came to the kids, we were able to pay the schools for lunch options to make sure that they didn't starve, and the mothers often didn't mind skipping a meal. We tried our best but exhausting funds didn't help when we needed those to help with medical bills, the rent, food, and staff.

Chapter 10

Alisha

I ARRIVED AT THE restaurant and hesitated before leaving the car. My phone was clutched in my hand, and I kept looking at it even though no one from Zohran Tech had ever, nor would ever message. It was a stupid thing to get hung up on, but I found myself looking anyway.

My grandmother was waiting at our usual booth, and she grinned when she saw me walking toward her.

"Little bird! I haven't seen you in forever," she exclaimed when I bent to hug her. "How's married life treating you, sweetheart?"

I shrugged my shoulders, but I couldn't go without answering her question not when the regret for my aunt's situation was something that haunted her every time she saw Lena's scars. "It's alright, Gran. It's awkward but Avi hasn't been cruel to me."

Sympathy shone in her dark eyes, but she smiled as she picked up the menu. "It will be, dove. Each of us went through the same thing."

"Talon's been phoning a lot," I stated as I glanced over my menu. If it wasn't a phone call at night, then it was a check-in message in the morning. I could tell my marriage to Avi Zohran bothered him, and I was doing my best to reassure him. It was hard though, Talon suffered a lot more after what happened to Lena than the rest of us, purely because he'd been sixteen or seventeen at the time and old enough to know what really happened. I did my best to reassure him that Avi didn't seem to be like that, but it was hard when I hardly knew my husband myself.

A waiter was already on the way to get our order and when he arrived, I asked for a cappuccino to drink and then ordered the steak fettuccine.

"He's worried about you, little bird. You're the closest thing he has to a sister," my grandmother shrugged in response as the waiter took our menus. She always ordered the same thing, a dish with steak and vegetables.

"I know." We were born in different months and in different years, but somehow, both Tal and I ended up being born on a hunter's moon, which became a running joke in the family.

Gran and I continued to exchange small talk as we waited for our food and coffee, but it wasn't more than ten minutes before they arrived, and she asked the first of who knows how many questions she had in store for me.

"You mentioned something on the phone about a Gala for the charity. Have you got any set ideas about that?" Gran questioned and I nodded. "Is this going to happen before or after the event this weekend?"

I froze, looking up at her carefully. "There's an event this weekend?"

Gran hummed to herself, sipping on her cappuccino. "Don't tell me you forgot, little bird?" she teased.

My eyes narrowed slightly. Forgetting one of Gran's events was life-threatening; everyone knew better than to do that. She arched a brow when I took too long to respond, and I sipped my cappuccino to save myself a few moments. It was the time of the year when everyone's birthdays were over, so that wasn't the reason and Alison would've told me if there was a charity event because we could normally piggy-back on Gran's events. That meant that I had no idea, and no matter how long I stalled, I wouldn't be getting out of an interrogation.

An irritated sigh was my first sign. "You do remember the stipulations of your contract, little bird?"

I mulled over that then choked on another sip of my coffee, setting the cup down hard enough to make it clatter against its saucer. "Gran, you can't seriously be planning to have our first event this weekend?"

The contract, that *damn* contract, had one clause that I'd forgotten about because weddings often happened every two years. The clause was that I had to attend an event where they could announce to the public our nuptials. I scrambled for something to say while Gran looked at me with disapproval shining through her eyes.

"It's too soon; we haven't even been together for a month."

"It's the perfect time," she answered me, wrinkling her nose. "I can't stall for much longer. Next month there are three separate events, and if you want a day for the charity Gala then you're going to need to plan ahead. It's not easy planning a good party, you know."

"I know, but —" her finger wagged, interrupting me before I could come up with an excuse.

"I've already sent out all the invitations, little bird. Everything's been booked and the caterers already let me know that they've started on some of the meals."

The food in front of me didn't look appetizing as I fidgeted on my chair. "I just think you could've warned me about this. No one mentioned anything the date or anything. I don't have anything to wear." I frowned, then scooped up a forkful of pasta until Gran's next words froze me mid-bite.

"Nuh-uh, my heart," she said warningly. "I told your husband. Did he not say anything?"

My lips pursed and I set my fork down, glaring at my cell phone. This is what happens when you don't communicate things well. "I'll speak to him this evening."

"See that you do, dear," she smiled warmly, and her hand reached across the table for mine. "Miscommunications are part of the learning process."

My laugh wasn't amused.

"Avi?" I called, stepping into the house.

Kai and Silas were in the living room when I walked through, and my temper blazed at their sudden stillness. It reeked of guilt to me.

"Gentlemen," I murmured, an eyebrow raised. "I'm looking for my husband. Do either of you know where he might be?"

Relief flashed across Silas' face as his phone started to ring and he gave me a sheepish grin before running out of the room. I scoffed, but if I was being honest then he was probably the last person I wanted to ask if the answer was that my husband was with Maya.

My chest ached at the thought, and I tried to ignore the pinch as I turned to Kai.

"Kai? Please, it's urgent," I softened my voice, hoping the Navajo would understand. If what Maya had said about him was right, then chances are he also had to deal with a crazy traditional family. My grandmother considered her events a way of bringing the tribe back together.

The big, scary Navajo fidgeted as my eyes turned pleading and five minutes later, I was storming out of the house and toward a hunting cabin that was apparently on the edge of the property.

I don't know how long it took to get there, or how long it took for me to wait for him afterward but by the time that Avi's vehicle pulled up to the cabin, the sky was starting to grow dark.

"Avi?" I called the moment he stepped out of the vehicle.

His shoulders sagged when he saw me on the steps and I frowned, that wasn't the reaction I expected after he had me panting between his legs yesterday. Was I right about Maya and him?

"Now's not the best time, spitfire," he tried to brush me off, walking right past but I grabbed the sleeve of his jacket and he stilled at the slightest tug.

"I wanted to talk to you." I tugged on his sleeve gently until he faced me. Avi's eyes dragged across my figure and his expression tightened. My brow furrowed. Why is he acting so strange?

"Can it not wait until tomorrow? I'm tired." He frowned and I backed away, smelling alcohol on his breath. Right. Tired. Did he go out with someone? Kai and Silas normally went out with him if it was a business thing so who did he go out with? Maya?

"No, Avi. It can't wait until tomorrow. I had lunch with my grandmother today and she let me know that they're holding an event for us this weekend. She said she told you about it." I folded my arms and stared at him. There was a flicker of recognition in his eyes as he glanced down at me again, but he didn't say anything and I continued, watching him warily. "My family's very *specific* about the events that they hold. If this event is about announcing our marriage, then we have to attend. There's no getting out of it."

"I'm struggling to see what the problem is?" His eyebrow rose, that same arrogant expression that he wore during our wedding planning outings was on his face now and I ground my teeth as he suddenly smirked down at me.

"The problem is that you didn't say anything about it. If you knew about the event, then you should've told me." I bit out, trying to control my temper. A small voice in my mind told me I was overreacting, but I ignored it.

"I'm sorry, I didn't think it was that important." He shrugged casually, placing his hands in his pockets. My eyes narrowed on him, and I let out a breath.

"You didn't think it was important?" I asked, a single eyebrow raised.

"It's just an event. I go to hundreds of those a year." His voice was flat. Disinterested and I felt frustration bubbling. Why's he acting like this? I glanced at the hunting cabin behind me, my mouth pursed as the silence turned heavy.

"Is that all you came to find out?" Avi asked suddenly and my gaze flicked back to him.

Was that all I wanted to find out? No, I wanted to know why he was here instead of at the house, but I didn't know how to ask that because he was acting like an ass, and I had the slightest suspicion that it had to do with Maya.

The silence grew as I considered his question, tucking my hair behind my ear as I did. With the way he was acting, it would be better if I left and came back to speak to him at another time. Instead, I scuffed my shoes and then muttered. "You missed dinner."

A cool breeze blew past, and I shivered while he sighed, running his hands through his hair again. "I was busy, it happens."

"Tonight, or yesterday?" I countered, ignoring the second part of that sentence, and he shrugged.

"Both."

My scoff was loud, but I didn't know what to say. That he was lying? That was evident, even though when I peeked through my lashes, he looked far too sober for someone that was drinking. The truth was that I really didn't have anything to accuse him.

"Is there a problem, Alisha?" Avi asked as he walked toward me and for a moment, I thought I saw a flicker of that same interest that he looked at me with yesterday. I must have been imagining it because it was gone the next second and I backed up a step, my brow furrowed as I stared at my feet. Was there a problem? Maybe not. Maybe I was just being paranoid. "Look, if it's about what happened yesterday then I think we should talk." I let out a breath, nodding along. Talking is good.

"Yesterday was a mistake. I'm sorry that I did that," Avi finished, and I swung my gaze toward him, shocked.

"I don't understand?" I sputtered.

"What happened won't happen again." He shrugged his shoulders as if it really wasn't a big deal and maybe to him it wasn't, but not to me. Seven years with Avi had started to seem like a really good deal up until now.

"So, I was right, you were with Maya." I shot him a look of disgust.

"What?" he frowned, dragging his blue eyes to meet mine. My cheeks flushed at his attention, and I watched him drag his hand through his hair. "Yes, I was at work with Maya, but we were running through a few notes on the project."

"You smell like alcohol, Avi. Why were you drinking if you were just discussing the project?" I huffed, his explanation didn't make any sense and it was ridiculous that he was trying to do this right now.

Avi barked out a laugh. "Seriously? What the hell is with the interrogation? Since when you need to know everything, I'm doing?"

"I don't, but considering we're married—" My voice came out small and I tried to shake off the sudden bout of insecurity telling me that maybe I was wrong.

Avi interrupted before I could say anything more, his tone sharp. "It's a marriage of convenience, Alisha, don't you get that?"

A lump formed in my throat. "So yesterday at the office was just an act? Or no, wait. Is this just something you do often? What... did you get what you wanted from Maya after you left yesterday, is that what this is?" I raised an eyebrow, pretending it didn't hurt to hear what he was saying. Avi's jaw clenched and he looked away, not answering my question. I let out a bitter laugh. "You do realize that dating other women is against the contract, right?"

"I don't have time for this," he muttered, staring at the sky and a moment later he was trying to get past.

"Avi!" I snarled, smacking my hands on his chest. "You can't just walk past. Answer the question, are you in a relationship with Maya."

I couldn't read his expression and he clenched his jaw before turning toward me with a cruel smile. "Don't fool yourself into thinking this is a relationship, spitfire. It's a contractual obligation, anything that happens between us is just for the sake of the arrangement. Therefore, it doesn't really matter if I'm sleeping with someone else."

He hadn't actually admitted to anything, still. Something in me snapped with his words. It could've been his callous tone or the cruel tilt to his lips... or maybe it had nothing to do with that and everything to do with the fact that another person was treating me like property. Like something they could use and then leave when they didn't feel like it anymore. Either way, the anger bubbled to the surface and before I even thought about it, I raised my hand and slapped him.

Avi's jaw clenched and all that anger turned to regret. "Oh my god," I whispered in horror. I was just as bad as the man who hurt my aunt. "Oh my god. Avi, I didn't—"

His eyebrow rose, a mixture of shock and —surprisingly— amusement dancing in his ice-bright eyes when he murmured, "I hope you have a reason for that, beautiful, because when I get my hands on you..." my eyes widened and he trailed off, regret lining his face.

Frustration made me fold my arms and his eyes dragged down my figure again. Heat spiraled inside me, something I shouldn't have felt considering everything. "When you get your hands on me, you'll do what?"

He didn't answer, his expression distracted. In fact, if I didn't know any better, then I would say it was torn but why?

"You'll do what, Avi?" I hissed through gritted teeth. "What were you going to say, Avi?"

Still nothing.

Damn him.

"Avi!" I snarled, and he smirked, glancing away.

"Nothing," he said before turning back toward the hunting cabin.

"Where are you going?" I shouted, stomping after him. We weren't even done with the conversation! Avi tried to close the door and I smacked my hands against it, not realizing he wasn't behind it until it slammed into the wall. I would regret that later, but for now I turned to Avi and shouted. "Avi! I swear to God if you don't answer me right now—"

"Answer which question? You're going to need to be a little more specific, spitfire, I've barely had a chance to speak after all your accusations," he drawled, running his fingers through his hair, then he pulled them out on a groan and turned toward the rest of the room before I could even answer him.

"Why the hell are you sleeping here instead of in the house?" I repeated slowly, breathing through my nose.

"You forget," he stated, turning to face me again. "This is my property, *wife*. Marrying me doesn't make it yours. I don't need to answer you."

Pain thumped behind my ribcage. He'd basically just confirmed what I thought. I was nothing more than property to men like him. It hurt, but it was easy to turn the pain into anger instead, and I took a step forward and snarled. "Maybe you're the one forgetting, Avi, because the contract clearly stated that this relationship is monogamous. If you're hiding up here just to fuck another woman, then I won't need that stupid arrangement to make you regret that."

Avi scratched the at his o'clock shadow but stayed quiet. Did he even realize he was swaying? How drunk was he and why didn't he just get a lift home if that was the case? I let out an irritated snarl and whipped off my high heels, throwing them in his direction but they landed every except where I wanted them to, and Avi only grew more amused.

"You should work on your aim, spitfire," he smirked. I couldn't deal with this tonight. This man was going to make me pull out my hair. I let out a scream.

"Fuck you!" I snarled, heading for the door. Let him sleep it off; I'll speak to him tomorrow.

"Alisha!" Avi called, and I heard something clatter as tears pressed against my eyeballs.

Fuck him.

Chapter 11

Alisha

I SHOULDN'T HAVE THROWN my high heels. The forest floor was filled with sharp debris that made me hiss as the sensitive skin under my feet split. It hurt, but so did my feelings, and feeling sorry for myself wasn't going to get me out of this mess. I had to get back to the house. At least Ora would be waiting for me. We could have a girl's night in, Avi had to have a can of tuna or something in the pantry I could use to bribe her with. Hell, why should I worry about tuna? I'm sure she'd like a piece of steak or something too.

"This is my property," I mocked under my breath, my thighs starting to burn as I climbed up the hill and toward the house. Why the hell hadn't I taken a car? There had to be a road leading to the hunting cabin, Avi's SUV drove right up to the front porch before he parked it. "Marrying me doesn't make it yours. I don't need to answer you."

If that was the case then I shouldn't have to answer to him either but instead, my whole life now revolved around Avi's decisions. Wake up, eat, go to work, come home, eat, go to bed... do everything pre-approved by my husband... and the whole time he'd been with *her*.

And what about the event planned for this weekend? We had to go, there was no getting out of it— but if we did go then I would have to pretend that things were okay otherwise Tal would start getting suspicious. A lump in my throat made me swallow. It's fine. Everything was fine. People weren't going to expect us to be in love already. Just a few months had passed, that wasn't enough time. Except... what if Tal started asking questions? He'd be there. I hadn't been lying about the cell phone calls, and getting through those was like having to stumble through the Spanish Inquisition. I couldn't. Not with Talon. There had to be a way to get Gran to cancel.

"Where's Tal when I need him," I sniffed, quickly wiping away the lone tear that fell.

They were blurring my eyes, forcing me to slow down. I didn't want to be stuck out here when the sunset. Navajo or not, I had no clue how to survive out in the wilderness. The little lessons that we learned on our annual camping trip meant nothing out here. What the hell would I do if a cougar stumbled across me?

I let out a self-deprecating laugh that quickly changed to a shriek when something slammed into me, throwing me right off my feet. The scream was cut short when I realized that I wasn't falling to the hard ground to be eaten by a cougar or some other wild beast.

"Stubborn fucking woman," Avi hissed, his strong arms coiled around me bridal style. I nearly let out another laugh at the irony, but I couldn't when I was still trying to catch my breath. "I'm going to spank your ass blue. What the fuck were you thinking? Who the hell walks around a forest barefoot? Fucking mad woman."

The warmth of his chest was enough to keep me quiet until he called me mad. Why did men always do that when we thought for ourselves? I wriggled in his grip, trying to break loose and when he wouldn't let me go, I snarled. "Dammit, Avi! I don't have the patience for this Avi. Let me go. Now, for crying out loud."

He grunted when my elbow hit his chest. "For fuck's sake, Alisha."

I shrieked again as he quickly changed his hold, throwing me over his shoulder like a sack of potatoes. Fiery pain on my ass shocked me silent, and his palm smacked me again before gripping on tight. "Move again, spitfire and I'll make sure your ass is so blue tomorrow that you won't be able to sit during the morning meetings."

His snarled words should've disgusted me, what the hell kind of caveman spanks a grown woman like she's a child anyway? Except, the idea of him bending me over something made my thighs clench instead, and that fiery pain from my ass spread toward another place entirely.

No, *damn it*. I didn't have time for those kinds of thoughts. "You don't get to say that, Avi! I'm just a contractual obligation, remember!" I spat out, fighting to get off. "Put me down, Avi!"

"Avi, I'm serious, put me down!" I cried out, smacking against his back. My efforts were in vain, and the squeal I let out when he slapped my ass cheeks only made the heat between my legs grow. This was so messed up.

Clearly, I hadn't gotten very far because less than a moment later my breath was knocked from me as Avi jogged up the hunting cabin's porch steps. Fuck, what now?

At least he wasn't drunk anymore. I stayed silent as he shut the door, and then moved to the table in the middle of the room. It was filled with papers, pizza boxes, and different mugs and plates. An indication that he'd been staying here a while, although, I didn't really need that clue. I figured that out myself after talking to Kai. I should've been relieved, but the thought turned my stomach sour. Was he really that turned off by me that he would rather break the contract than sleep with me? Or was it his relationship with Maya? Were they that serious? The contract didn't allow for that. This marriage had to be monogamous otherwise we would both lose out.

With one arm holding me in place, Avi quickly used his free hand to push the papers aside, throw the pizza boxes on the floor, and then quickly move the dishes from the table to the kitchen island. I grimaced. No doubt where they'd stay until someone came in to clean up for him. That was just like everyone else in my family. They thought that because they had money to pay people to do the shit work, then they wouldn't have to do it themselves.

I scowled up at him when he finally sat me on the edge of the table. It was no use though; he wasn't even looking. My breath faded when he crouched, pulling each foot up for inspection until he let them go gently, watching them swing.

"You've cut your feet," he informed me icily, and then the next thing I knew, he was striding toward a door on the far side of the room. "Don't fucking move."

I rolled my eyes but stayed in place, glancing around the room. Could Maya have been right about the women he'd been with? Did he bring her here to fuck her on the couch? The L-shaped leather couch looked similar to the one I had in my apartment; the only difference was the lack of throw pillows to soften the area. Instead, there was a blanket and two pillows.

The couch didn't have any side tables but right behind it, on the longer side, there was a long table that looked custom-made. It stood just a bit lower than the edge of the couch and on it was Avi's laptop, briefcase, and a few remotes. One likely for the huge TV on the wall, although I had trouble thinking he ever used it.

Avi didn't strike me as the type to binge-watch a TV series on an off day. The man was always too busy with work to do something so casual.

I glanced around the rest of the room, taking in the dark decor and spotting a few telltale signs that Avi had been up here all week. His shoes were near the door, the ties on the coat rack, and a clean set of work shirts on the kitchen island. Did this place not have a bedroom?

There were two doors on the far side of the room, the one Avi had gone through earlier was open, and a white light inside lit up to show the bathroom. That explained what room that was, but what about the other? Surely, he hadn't been sleeping on the couch?

Cupboard doors slammed shut and I blinked, watching Avi as he came out of the bathroom with a first aid kit in his hand. His jaw was clenched, and his eyes were icy as he glared at me.

"I didn't ask you to bring me here," I snapped, folding my arms over my chest defensively. What was it about him that always made me say and do stupid shit that I normally wouldn't say or do?

"So, I should've just let you walk back to the house with your feet bleeding?" he bit out before crouching in front of me once more.

"They aren't bleeding," I scoffed, earning another glare.

"Take a look if you don't believe me, princess. Another twenty minutes of walking and you wouldn't be able to wear those heels you like so much," he growled, sounding so put out that I wanted to smack him. I never once asked him to look after me. Yet, I couldn't, because the next thing I knew I was biting on my lip to keep myself from crying out as he wiped antiseptic over the bottom of my feet.

I whimpered before I could stop myself and Avi froze. I couldn't help the noise, it burned. God, it burned really bad.

"Stop that!" Avi snapped suddenly, and I flinched at his vicious tone. "Keep crying like that and I'll give you a damn good reason to whine."

"You don't have to be such an asshole!" I snapped back. He knew exactly what to say to make me feel like a child. I ripped my foot out of his hand, but Avi grabbed it a second later, palm smacking once sharply against my bare thigh. "It burns!" I shouted, jerking my foot away from him again, then before he could retaliate, I quickly got on my hands and knees to crawl away from him.

"Keep still, damn it!" Avi snapped, his hands finding my hips and before I could even protest, he pulled me back into place.

"No!" I growled, struggling to move away. "I'm not going to sit here while you treat me like a child. I'm not a child!"

"I didn't say you were, I said you were an obligation," he snapped, and I let out another shriek, fingers reaching for my hair.

"Contract or not, *I'm your wife, Avi!*"

Avi's dark glare made my own eyes narrow, but before I could snarl something, else he leaned in and bit out, "Trust me, I fucking know."

I reared back to blink at him in shock. "What the hell does that mean?" My voice was terse. This man was giving me a headache as I tried to keep up with him.

"It means that you're going to sit still so that I can clean your pretty, bleeding feet because you shouldn't have been in the forest anyway, but if you'd rather act like a spoiled brat then I'll treat you like a spoiled brat," Avi answered and with burning cheeks I did exactly that. I kept still, watching him go onto his knees once more to clean my feet and after he bandaged them, Avi rose back to his full height and offered me his hand. His mask was once more in place as he helped me off the table.

"Where are you going?" I asked as he let me down and left me standing in the middle of the room.

"I'm getting my keys to take you back to the house," he said without any emotion, and after doing exactly that, he stood by the door and glanced over at me with a cool expression. "Let's go."

Panic entered my bloodstream. I didn't want to go back to the house with him because it was obvious he was just going to come back. His laptop was still near the couch, and Avi didn't go anywhere without the damn thing. Still, how the hell did I explain to him that I didn't want to be left alone in that huge house? Ok, fine. Kai and Silas wouldn't have left. Maybe. Still.

"No," I supplied quickly, and before he could fetch me and physically take me out of the hunting cabin with him, I walked toward the couch and sat down. It smelled of him. I sniffed as discretely as possible. The bed in our room smelled just as good until Rosa cleaned the sheets.

"What do you mean *no*?" Avi snapped, closing the door again.

"I don't want to go back," I answered him simply, my gaze roaming around the room. There wasn't anything personal inside. It really was just a hunting cabin.

"You're going back, Spitfire, I don't have time for this."

"No," I replied again, folding my arms across my chest as Avi stood there, jaw clenched, and fingers wrapped tight around the keys. That expression on his face, the darkness and annoyance used to make me close up but after a few weeks with him, I started to get a flick of pleasure anytime his cold facade started to crack.

"We're married," I reminded him with a haughty expression. Then I crossed my legs and started to examine my fingernails as if I were bored. "I still want an explanation regarding why you're staying in a hunting cabin instead of in the main house with me."

Trying to hide my amusement, I watched Avi grind his teeth hard enough to make a muscle in his cheek pop with every back-and-forth motion.

Something must've shown on my face because, in the next moment, Avi started to slowly prowl closer, and he didn't stop until he was right in front of me. "Alisha," he drawled, and I got a stronger whiff of his cologne. "I don't have the patience to deal with this tonight. Now, get up and walk to the car."

So, when he said it then it was okay? Pretending to think about it, I hummed quietly. "Nope."

His eyes flashed. Gorgeous blue eyes that looked like lightning when they snapped toward me like that. I should've taken it as a warning, should've known not to push his boundaries but after everything... after working my ass off, and trying to cook, after the charity benefit and the photos in the media. After everything that happened these last few weeks, I didn't have the energy in me to give a shit if he lost his temper. It was a long time coming, anyhow.

Of course, I didn't expect him to place his big hands on my waist and pull me straight off the couch.

"What are you—" I didn't get to finish the question either before I was forced onto all fours, my legs between his and my torso shoved onto the couch. Slight pressure on my upper back made my breath hitch and I wouldn't admit it but when his fingers tugged up my skirt, I widened my legs in preparation. Except it wasn't what I was expecting and I only realized what was happening when his hand landed on my ass, faster and harder than before.

I screamed at the fiery burst of heat. "Avi, what the fuck!"

He kept at it, smacking each ass cheek until I was squirming. "Spoilt fucking brat, can't you just listen when you're told?" His palm cracked against my bare ass again and again, only deviating to switch sides or change the pattern.

"Shit, stop! Stop, I'm sorry," I squirmed, trying to pull away because it really felt like he was about to make good on his promise from earlier. "Avi!"

He stopped after my whine and I let out a breath, sinking into the couch. My ass was on fire, and my cheeks were red but worse than all of that was the realization that he could see everything from where he was crouched behind me.

I stopped breathing when his fingers slipped under the top of my panty, the touch feather soft after the slaps he'd delivered just a second ago, but it burned just the same. He slid that finger down, pulling my underwear with him and my breath started on a stutter as I squeezed my eyes shut. I already knew what he'd see after pulling them down to my knees, but the quiet curse from his lips shattered me.

"Fuck."

Avi widened my legs, his one hand a pressure between my shoulder blades again as he slowly but surely started to rub against the wetness that was spreading from my pussy to my ass.

His finger didn't breach past my pussy lips but slid along the outside then up to the rim of my asshole. He circled it, his breath heavy behind me and I whimpered, my eyes wide as I froze in place. He wouldn't.

The air was tense as he seemed to think about doing exactly that, but then he dragged his fingers down again, sliding them through my pussy lips and toward my clit. The moment he touched it, I jumped, a strangled noise leaving my lips and that was enough to break whatever the fuck had been holding him in place.

"Fuck," Avi groaned, before thrusting his fingers into me. "You're soaking wet, princess. Did you like my hand on your ass?"

I whimpered, arching my back as he thrust his fingers in and out again.

"Answer me, Alisha." he stopped thrusting, leaving my whole body tight and waiting. I couldn't say what he needed me to, the admission lay thick within my throat and Avi seemed to sense that because he returned to what he was doing, fingers thrusting into me and curling. "Don't you want to come, princess?"

My body was molten lava under his fingers, and he let go to smooth his hands over my burning ass cheeks. "I'll make you feel so good, Alisha."

No, I shook my head only to scream as his palm smacked my sore ass again. Then he smoothed over the heat, fingers returning to my pussy. Fuck it felt so good when he thrust into me like that, curling his fingers up until they brushed against something deep inside of me. I let out a long, drawn-out moan and arched up once more only to scream in fury when he left my pussy to smack me again.

Avi laughed at me, and I turned to glare over my shoulder. His eyes were molten when he met my gaze and he pulled his sticky fingers into his mouth and sucked, hard. My pussy clenched at the gesture, but he didn't move his fingers back to it like he had each time before. No, instead they went back to that part of me that he shouldn't ever be touching, and they circled around and around.

"Lie to me again and I'll fuck your pretty ass instead of smacking it," he threatened, and the look in his eyes told me he meant it. "Now answer me properly, princess. Do you want to come?"

He held my gaze, those fingers pressing against the soft, sensitive skin until it threatened to give way. Fuck, I couldn't, just the thought of what it might feel like to have him *there* of all places made shivers trail down my spine.

"Yes," I gave in, then nearly wept when he pushed me onto my back and spread my thighs wide.

A second later Avi was licking my pussy, his eyes dancing with amusement as I struggled to catch my breath. While he licked and sucked, his fingers were pressing my thighs down and opening me up more. My eyes nearly rolled back into my head as he moved his tongue toward my entrance and licked every bit of the cream coming out of me.

Chapter 14

Avi

I DIDN'T STAND A chance after carrying her back to the hunting cabin. Alisha's breasts pressed against my shoulder left me raging, and my palm on her backside only made my dick throb harder.

Cleaning her feet was a courtesy, but fuck, I should've known what it would do to me just having her sitting with her skirt flashing me those creamy white panties every time I bent to pick them up. But then I caught sight of what they looked like and had to stop myself from turning her around right then and there so that I could spank some sense into her.

Her feet were fucked; I don't know how she managed to walk for a solid ten minutes without me finding her, but she wouldn't have made it to the house even if she figured out, she was going in the wrong direction.

The plan had been to just clean them up and take her back, but then she had to go and get mouthy. It shouldn't have been surprising, ever since I made her clean the coffee she spilled in my office, she'd been getting braver and braver.

Now I had her laying on her back on my couch, legs spread and pussy glistening just for me, and I forgot the exact reasons why I shouldn't pull my dick out and dip it in. Just the tip, I snickered, eyes glancing toward her pebbled nipples. There was no fucking way I'd be able to leave it at just the tip, not with her red-cheeked and panting.

Edging her was cruel, but it was nothing compared to the blue-balls I'd had the past few weeks. I bent to nip at her clit, enjoying her scream until she stopped trying to hold herself up to watch and instead tried to get a grip on my hair.

"Nuh-uh," I warned, letting go of her thigh to spank that little clit.

Alisha hissed, arching her back. "Avi!"

"Only good girls can pull my hair, princess," I grinned, pressing a hand on her stomach before I pushed the fingers on my other hand into her wet heat. A moan left my lips. "Fuck, you're tight, baby. I don't think I'll even be able to fit."

I was teasing, but seeing the frustration on her face made me think that even if I didn't fit, we'd figure out how to get me in. Alisha was as desperate as me, sweat beading on her top lip as she writhed on my couch.

"You want my cock, baby girl?"

Hearing her whimper was music to my ears and I let go to unzip and pull myself out, seeing her lick her lips as my fingers tightened around the base of my cock and pumped straight toward my crown. She'd look good with those pretty pink lips wrapped around my cock.

"Avi," she panted, and I backed a step away, enjoying the frustration that crossed over her features.

"Strip."

The panty was first, Alisha tore it off before she even wiggled out of her dress, leaving it pooled by the side of the couch and I grinned. There was no going back now. Her slim fingers unhooked her bra and my mouth dried up as her breasts bounced, nipples pebbled and rosy.

"Pinch them," I demanded, glaring at her when she looked at me uncertainly. Her fingers quickly went to each breast, pinching the nipples. "Harder, baby, and then keep them there for me while I fuck my dick against your clit."

Alisha moaned, leaning back with her legs spread and ready for me to do exactly that. I approached her quickly, pushing myself between her legs until her pussy was bared obscenely. Then I thrust against her with a grunt, feeling the tip of my crown against her pebbled clit.

The sound she made was feral. She keened, and I snapped.

Alisha

My whole body went taught when Avi thrust into me, his thick cock ramming straight past my virginity and the snap of pain made me squeal and tighten. Of course, it was nothing compared to how tense he was when he figured it out.

"Please tell me you weren't a fucking virgin," Avi gritted out, his whole body frozen.

It took me a while to respond, I was too busy breathing through the pain and fullness of having him so deep inside of me. What the fuck was I thinking? Egging him on like that?

"Alisha!" he snapped, drawing my attention to him.

I wanted to cry at the look on his face. The darkness I thought was lust suddenly looked very different with the realization that he'd just taken my virginity in one thrust. Fuck, fuck, fuck.

He started to pull away, his slick cock slick hard and unyielding.

"Avi, wait!" I begged, clinging to that feeling. Maybe the pain had been a bit much at first, but it was going away and now there was an ache inside of me that wanted more.

"Don't go," I pleaded, wrapping my body against his. He still had his pants on, and while I'd been surprised at first that he went to work without any underwear, I was grateful for it. The relief was short-lived, and I panted again as heat curled low in my belly, aided by the feel of him sinking into me again.

"I should've smacked your ass harder," he grunted, glaring at me through his slow thrust.

"Next time," I promised, losing myself to the feel of him inside of me. There was so much heat, I widened my legs, and he sank deeper, causing my pussy to clench. I didn't even realize what I said until a few minutes had passed.

Avi grunted, his eyes turning feral as he leaned back to watch himself. I watched too, turned on by the sight of his strong thighs knocking into me until my breasts bounced, but it wasn't enough, and I started to wiggle in place, knocking my hips clumsily against his.

I didn't have rhythm, not like he did but I still managed to get him to lose focus, and he sank into me with a drawled curse. "Fuck."

"Avi," I begged, still trying to move under his weight.

"Tell me what you need," he whispered, cradling me like I was something precious. A sob caught in my chest as my emotions strung themselves together. I cradled him with my hips, legs hooked over his waist until my ankles were crossed. Wasn't it clear to him?

"Everything," I whispered, the word meaning more than I allowed it to, but my clumsy attempt was enough to get him to move, and I let out a high-pitched moan when he started to fuck me harder.

"Avi," I panted, reaching toward him. He let me pull myself up until I could kiss and suck on his neck and that's where I stayed until he knocked something inside of me that made the slow, spiraling heat burst like a firecracker in my veins.

I shrieked, clenching my thighs around his hips until he was forced to stay inside me with every clenching moment of that orgasm. His breath scattered goosebumps across my neckline, and my whole body shivered. God, I wanted to bury myself in his scent.

When my clenching stopped, Avi picked up his pace, hands moving to my hips where he lifted them for more support and my cheeks burned at the sounds we were making. His skin smacking against mine and that wet sucking when he upped his pace, but my attention was diverted a moment later when Avi grunted, and I felt heat rushing into my sore and aching pussy.

"Shit," he whispered as I breathed into that place where his shoulder met his neck. He pulled us up from the couch, and I shivered in the cold air, hugging myself to him tighter.

I can't believe we just did that, I thought, slightly shocked.

A door opened and I breathed in his scent as my eyes started to close. Avi set me on the bed and pulled away, the sensation making me hiss.

I opened my eyes and watched him walk out of the room, unable to say anything as pain struck me deep in my soul. I turned on my side, feeling tears press against my eyelids but I had no energy to sob.

"Fuck, are you crying?" Avi muttered from the doorway, an expression of horror on his face. I blinked, seeing the cloth in his hands and feeling like an idiot. There was no point in lying though, not when a tear fell with that blink and dripped down my cheek.

"Alisha," he said hoarsely, walking toward me. "Why are you crying?"

My lip wobbled, and I shrugged before admitting in a weak voice. "I didn't know what to think."

"About?"

"You haven't been at the house all week and then we— and you just walked out," I hiccupped, hating myself for the weakness in my voice and the tears dripping down my face. God, I pushed my hands against my closed eyes as if that would stop the tears pouring down my cheek. Not now. God, not now.

"Open your legs," Avi demanded, and I paused my sniffling to watch as he wiped the cloth against my used pussy. There was a bit of blood on it, and he grimaced at the sight. "I never planned for this."

"I know," I admitted as another lump formed in my throat. Laying on the bed in front of him, I could see a bit of blood smeared from his cock to his thigh, and that only hit home how much I fucked up. Avi didn't want a 23-year-old wife; his actions over the past few weeks had shown as much. I was just a business transaction, and I shouldn't have taken things as far as I did.

"What are you thinking," he asked, throwing the cloth on the other side of the room. I hesitated, unable to voice the question in my mind. "You're going to have to spell it out for me, princess. I don't know what's going on, I can't read your mind." His fingers trailed to the back of my neck, and he started to massage it.

A sticky laugh left my lungs, the sound as bittersweet as the sight of my husband admitting he didn't know what to do with me. I didn't know either, so I wasn't sure what he thought speaking about it would help.

"We didn't use protection," I whispered instead, and when he froze, I wanted to snatch the words straight back from the air. God, I was such an idiot, this whole thing was stupid and the sight of him there in front of me made me vulnerable.

He didn't say anything else, but he didn't leave either, and I stopped crying, but I didn't stop feeling like a fool as he lay next to me. Avi was older, with a body like a god and a business he'd been running since his twenties. I didn't have his life experience, and up until tonight, I'd been a virgin with lusty thoughts and no backbone to follow through on them.

Eventually, my thoughts settled, and I fell asleep.

Avi was gone when I woke.

I shouldn't have been surprised, but it didn't stop me from feeling used like something he'd purchased at an auction, a piece of art to display on his arms and then never take out again. My chest felt raw with feeling, and when I crawled out of bed, I realized the rest of me was aching too.

There was a bathroom in his hunting cabin, and I walked to it, wincing with each step. I didn't know what I was thinking. How could I have been so naive that I honestly thought having sex with him would mend the bridge between us? There was still so much we didn't know about each other. I didn't know how to be a good wife to my husband, and I was getting tired of trying.

I ignored the mirror and opened the tap for the shower, waiting for the warm water to sputter and fill the bathroom with steam. Then I got in, my bottom lip caught between my teeth as my muscles relaxed. I was such an idiot. I leaned against the wall until the cool tile met my forehead, hoping the water could drown out the memories of feeling him around me. In me. God, I was an idiot. I honestly thought sex would help, but now it felt like I'd made it all worse. How the fuck was I going to face him after crying last night?

Maybe he ran away because he thought I didn't want it? Or maybe he just left because he realized how much work I was.

A touch against my neck brought me out of my thoughts, and I felt my breath catch. "Avi?"

"Were you expecting someone else, spitfire?" he whispered, breath teasing the skin below my jaw.

"N—No," I stuttered while heat moved to my face.

A quiet hum answered me a moment before his hands settled on my hip, turning me to face him, and I squeezed my eyes shut without thinking.

"What, no clever comeback today?" he murmured the question and I swallowed, unable to answer him. "Look at me, Alisha."

My eyes opened without my saying so and ended up clashing with the blue of his. This was all too much. "What do you want, Avi?" I questioned as my hands came up to his chest, my skin a lot darker than his. Another difference. There were so many... I don't know why I honestly thought that this would work out.

Amusement curled his lips as he bent his head toward mine. "Right now? I just want to kiss my wife."

My breath caught a second before his lips landed on mine but then he pulled away with a sigh. "We need to talk."

"Now?" I murmured, I hadn't even had a chance to wash yet, and Avi muttered a curse before bending to kiss my neck.

"After the shower," he promised before pressing me against the wall and kissing me senselessly. Then he pulled away again, grabbed his shampoo, and told me to rinse my hair.

I had a silly grin on my face by the time we got out, my body still tingling from where his hands had caressed my skin.

"I didn't sleep with Maya," he murmured, plucking a towel from the rail. His eyes were exhausted as he wrapped it around himself and grabbed a second for me.

"I shouldn't have accused you," I shook my head, feeling ashamed. "I'm sorry, Avi. I don't know what came over me."

"Looked a lot like jealousy to me," he teased, pulling me in for another kiss and then breaking away. "But we really need to talk, come on."

I followed him to the bedroom and Avi pulled out one of his shirts for me to wear, then got dressed in boxers and tugged me by the hand to the kitchen. I grimaced, it really was a mess on this side and what we'd done earlier only made it worse.

"Sit," he pointed to the couch, then moved toward the kitchen. I only realized when he came back that he must've gone to grab food because he was carrying two plates piled high with what smelled like Rosa's spaghetti. My stomach grumbled and I mumbled a thank you before digging in. "My grandfather arranged this marriage."

"I know." I glanced up at him, remembering what my grandfather said in that meeting.

"Yes, but you don't know why it was arranged like this," he pointed out, setting his plate on the coffee table and running his hands through his wet hair. I didn't like not meeting his eyes, but I stayed still while he continued. "Before I was born, my grandfather arranged my father's marriage with one of your aunts."

I narrowed my eyes. Which aunt?

"Lena," he answered understanding my question. My eyebrows raised. Lena?

"That's not possible, Lena got married when I was 8," I answered, shaking my head.

"She was supposed to be married before that. To my father," he raised his head, meeting my gaze. "Lena Altaha was the first bridge arranged to marry a Zohran; I still have a copy of the agreement they signed."

"They signed it," I echoed, my brow furrowed. "I don't understand." If she had chosen not to marry his father, then Lena would've been cut off. That couldn't have happened because she got married when I was 8.

"A week before the wedding, my father's high school sweetheart came back into his life and he chose to marry her instead, but my grandfather didn't approve of the engagement, and they eloped—"

"Which is a direct violation of the contract," I finished.

He nodded his head, "Yes, and my grandfather couldn't do anything because my mother was pregnant with me at the time."

So *that's what happened to Bella Hayes.*

"But the contract was signed, and because of that, your grandfather wanted to make sure he got his end of the bargain. However, the timing wasn't always right. Twelve years ago, I would've been married to someone else in your family, if your grandfather hadn't gotten a business opportunity that was bigger than our business had been at the time," Avi explained, and I frowned.

Twelve years ago, one of my cousins had married into a Turkish family with ties to a few very important political figures. Supposedly, but then it came out that while they were rich, they had no ties to any political families and Grandfather lost out. He was furious at the time, and because of that, he'd lost the privilege of choosing the arrangements. My father was voted in, instead.

"After a while, our technology started getting better, and we became an industry leader in several areas. Tao realized that he'd missed out and contacted my grandfather multiple times over the years to arrange another contract. Every single time my grandfather declined due to bad blood. Things changed when he was diagnosed with leukemia. At the moment, I'm my grandfather's only heir and he isn't happy about that," Avi stretched his hand toward me, tucking a piece of hair behind my ear. "If he dies tomorrow, then one of his brother's kids, or grandkids will inherit the family fortune. Included in that is Zohran Tech. The only way to change that was if I started my own family."

Everything was starting to make sense. Why my grandfather had been involved. Why the wedding was so rushed... If Heinrich only figured out about his leukemia this year, then I was chosen to get married because I was the eldest unmarried granddaughter at the time.

Avi's phone started ringing, and I watched him absent-mindedly, my appetite gone as I considered it all. It made sense. It really did, but there was still something missing. Why was Avi going along with everything when he was the CEO of the company and not his grandfather? If the problem was inheriting Zohran Tech, then why not just take it out of the will and give it to Avi now? Why keep it in there?

There had to be more to the story, but the cell phone interrupted. Avi gave me a questioning glance, and when I nodded, he answered it.

"Avi, speaking."

I watched his body tense, and I frowned, setting my pasta on the table.

"There has to be a mistake," he stated, shaking his head. "No. I refuse to hear it. I want to see proper evidence." His face paled and for the first time ever, I witnessed Avi Zohran become speechless.

Chapter 15

Alisha

THE SILENCE IN THE office was heavy when Avi, and I walked in the next morning. No one had slept after hearing the news. No one could believe it, but Maya's phone call confession was played on speaker in the room between Avi and me the same way he played it now with Kai and Silas to hear it too.

Both had their head in their hands. Both were shaking, just like Avi had been when he heard the news. My heart was breaking for all of them, but it was breaking for Maya as well and her sobs echoed through Avi's top-floor office.

"I'm sorry, I had to. I didn't know what to do. I couldn't tell Silas; I couldn't tell any of you. I was scared, Avi. Please understand. Please don't hate

me. I didn't know what to do," her cries were soft, and my heart ached for the girl I called friend.

"*I'm trying to understand, Maya. I'm trying but you need to explain it to me.*" Avi's voice was hoarse. This part of the recording had come after he'd pleaded with the security and police officers to let her go.

"*He— I thought he loved me,*" Maya whispered, her voice cracking halfway through.

"*My grandfather doesn't love anyone. You should've known that.*" Avi answered, his voice ice-cold. As cold as his expression when he said it. As cold as he'd been since he heard her confession.

"*I do now,*" she wailed, sobs coming through the line. "*I don't know what to do. Please, Avi. I don't know how to be a mother. I didn't want this.*"

My mouth thinned, and I turned my watering eyes to the skyline instead. It shouldn't have been possible, yet it happened. Maya fell in love with Avi's grandfather, and after finding out that she was pregnant, he made her a promise that they were going to get married and be together. Then she lost the baby and he started to blackmail her to get more information about Avi. In return, Maya had been leaking information about Zohran Tech.

Silas was shaking, his face green after hearing his sister's confession, and when Avi glanced at him, he stood up and started pacing. His hands were in his hair, tugging and pulling. "I didn't know, man. God! I didn't know. She was acting weird, but I thought it was just because she was tired."

Kai lifted his head and stared at the phone with a broken expression. I wished I could go and hug each of them but when I tried that with Avi last night, he pulled away and hasn't looked at me since. I understood some part of it, the realization that I didn't know enough about Avi and this little family he's built to really understand the betrayal. Yet, on some level, I did get the betrayal too. How many times did I isolate myself just to try and cover up the hurt from hearing I was just another business transaction to my family? Wasn't that the same in a way?

Then there was Maya.

Avi, Kai, and Silas didn't know but she was at Lena's until this got sorted out. I phoned my aunt the second Avi walked out of the hunting cabin. The last thing I wanted was to wake up tomorrow and hear that she'd committed suicide after confessing. What Maya did was terrible but there was more to the story and the guys were too close to see it.

Lena was going to cover her legally, but there was also a therapist that I asked Lena to persuade Maya to see. All signs pointed to a verbally, and possibly even physically abusive relationship and I felt guilty that I didn't recognize it that day when Heinrich and Maya were right in front of me. I wish I'd known her well enough then to realize she was covering up post-partum depression.

Silas started to cry when Avi walked over, and I watched them warily as my husband set a hand on his shoulder. I couldn't hear what was said but Silas' shoulders only shook more before he walked out.

"Where's he going?" Kai demanded, shaking himself out of his stupor.

"I told him to go home. It's better if he isn't here at the moment," Avi responded flatly, his gaze on me for the first time since he pulled away yesterday. God, there was so much pain in his eyes, and I glanced outside the window again. I wished there was enough history between us that he would listen because the second I realized what he said, I felt sick. He was making a mistake.

"You can't blame Si for this, Avi," Kai snarled, reaching out to push at his chest. "What the fuck are you doing?"

"I'm making sure my company is alright," Avi growled in response as he shook off Kai's grip.

"You're making a mistake," Kai snapped before walking off. He glanced at me on his way out, but I could tell he didn't even see me.

I glanced outside the window again when he left. I didn't know what to do, my phone had been silent since Maya, and I chatted last.

I fell asleep on the couch at some point, and when I woke, Avi was standing by the windows with a tumbler of whiskey in his hands. It was early in the morning, much earlier than I'd ever been awake and hints of the sun were just starting to peak over the horizon, signaling a new day. A new day with a new beginning. One brought on by a friend's betrayal. I squeezed my eyes shut with a sigh before opening them to glance over at my husband again.

Avi stood there with shoulders slumped as he stared at the city skyline. I didn't know what to say, or how to take the weight off his shoulders but I found myself moving toward him anyway.

"You should go home," he murmured the moment my arms wrapped around his waist. "The press will be hounding the company as soon as the doors are open. I don't want you to have to deal with that."

"I'm not going anywhere." I stood behind him like I planned to stand behind him until this was sorted. "I promise."

And I didn't. I stayed with him in the office as the police came through and took his statement. I didn't move or say anything, but I nearly buckled in relief when he said he wasn't going to press charges against Maya.

I stayed with him as he let the staff know that the company would be temporarily shut down for two weeks while they updated the security systems and finalized the investigation. I was there when his grandfather came through, raging about the company's reputation and I hid a smile when Avi had the new security guards throw him out of the building.

My family phoned and messaged, offering me refuge in their homes until everything was sorted out and I declined, preferring to stay with Avi instead.

At first, I thought he would be alright. Avi threw himself into the company with a terrifying determination, but it worked because, with the new hires, Zohran Tech was starting to get back to where it was without any problems. Then everything went wrong.

My husband seemed to disappear right before my eyes as the months passed.

Before I even knew it, three months had come and gone since we found out about Maya's betrayal and Avi still didn't know that I was helping her. Mainly because he wasn't even home in the first place. I was at Lena's house, watching a movie with Tal, Lena, and Maya on the couch. I'd been here since the previous week's Sunday, carrying Ora in her cat carrier and phoning Lena with tears dripping down my face.

I hadn't told them why yet, because, in all honesty, I wanted to tell *him* first. The only problem was that four days had come and gone, and Avi didn't even know I wasn't at home because he hadn't left the office. He was sleeping elsewhere again, and I hated it, but I couldn't confront him because he was fighting his own battles.

Without his head engineer to take on the project, Avi hired multiple people to take on the role, working between departments to try and get the project finished. The last time I dropped in to make sure he was okay, that had been Saturday, and I'd had to walk around the sixteen floors of Zohran Tech just to find out that he was in the lab.

He looked like a stranger when I found him. His face was scruffy and shadowed, and he'd lost weight at some point. Depression did that to you though.

Kai hadn't been at the house when I came back, but he'd been looking more or less the same. Silas had moved out, and not even Maya could get ahold of him, so I ended up sending Lena a message. Her checks came back, he'd bought an apartment somewhere in California, but he wasn't doing any better than the rest of them.

Rosa was here with us at Lena's. She was the one to drive me to the hospital after I collapsed in the bathroom on Saturday after I came back from visiting Avi. She wasn't supposed to be working that weekend, but she'd been worried when the same thing happened on Wednesday. The second time it happened, she convinced me to go to the hospital. Then after we figured out what the problem was, Rosa was the one who drove me to Lena's, her tongue clucking the whole way.

"It's not right," she muttered, even now. We all winced as the pots clanged in the kitchen. "None of this is right. My Avi would've answered his phone by now." She wasn't the only one angry that he hadn't.

"Are you going to explain why she keeps doing that?" Maya whispered and three pairs of eyes glanced my way.

"Nope," I bit into a piece of popcorn, eyeing my traitor cat who slept in Talon's arms.

More pots clanged and everyone winced again.

Of course, that's when my cell phone started ringing. I let out a curse, dumping popcorn all over the blankets as I scrambled for the cell phone on the table. *Please, Avi. Please tell me it's you.*

It wasn't. My body deflated as I answered the phone.

"Hi, Alison."

My assistant's chirpy voice filtered through the phone as she let me know about this week's debrief but none of it seemed to matter anymore as I met Rosa's eyes across the room. Her head shook and I nearly started to cry again when I saw the tears glistening in her eyes. I didn't want to believe it either.

When I put the phone down and went to use the bathroom, my eyes were red-rimmed and tired in the mirror.

Rosa stood outside, shaking her head when I came out. "If you don't fetch him, *Mija*, then he's going to have a lot of regrets when he realizes."

I didn't want to go back to Zohran Tech yet though. Not when Avi couldn't even answer my last message to him. Instead, I walked back to the couch, my shoulders slumped as I waited for a response that wasn't going to come.

Alisha [3:45 p.m. Saturday, Mar 2nd]: Avi, you aren't picking up your phone. I'm at the hospital, please call me when you get this.

Alisha [1:15 a.m. Monday Mar 4th]: Avi, I'm pregnant.

I should've known that Talon would be the one to drag the information out of Rosa. I glared at his head.

Another week had passed and after forcing me to shower and get ready, my best friend was dragging me to Zohran Tech where Avi would inevitably be.

"You're an asshole," I said in a low voice as Tal drove, fingers tapping on the wheel. Avi was one too. Actually no, he wasn't. He was depressed, but nothing I'd said or done had pulled him from the brink and he'd chosen work over my worrying.

"And you're pregnant," Tal sang, but there was a bite to his normal humor. His eyes flicked over to me, and he grinned disparagingly. "As your emotional support uncle, it's my job to help you fix whatever *this*," he gestured toward me, "Is so that you can do all the happy mommy things you want to do."

The only thing that would make me a happy mommy right now was to sleep, something the doctor recommended over and over when I left the hospital two weeks ago. This should've been a joyous occasion, but it wasn't because according to the doctor, if I kept fainting from stress then I could lose the baby.

"Nuh-uh," Tal nudged my shoulder. "Don't you go and get depressed now too. We're going to fix this. I promise you."

Lena and Maya had opted to stay home for this day trip, and Rosa had to go home but she was shouting in Spanish at someone over the phone. I had an idea who it was, but even so, I doubt she would've been connected because he still hadn't returned anyone's messages.

Tal waved at the guards as he drove into the underground parking, whistling to himself before he stopped in front of the entrance and looked at me calmly. "Now what are you going to do?"

I let out a sigh before reiterating the words the whole house had been drilling into me when we started planning. "Find my husband, tell him the news, bring him home."

"And then what's going to happen?" Talon asked, an eyebrow raised defiantly.

"We're going to talk," I answered him, turning to stare at the empty car park. "And then we're going to find Silas, and Kai so that we can let them know about Maya's case."

Heinrich, the despicable bastard, was suing Maya for damages even though he'd left her with several mental scars and terrible depression.

"Goodie!" Tal shouted, then he leaned over and opened my door for me. "Out."

I grumbled before following his instruction, glaring at him the moment the door was closed, and he went to park it. The rule was that I wouldn't be going home until Avi left the building, which meant that if I didn't get the stubborn ass to let go of his multi-million—or billion—dollar project then I would be sleeping on the couch in his office tonight and eating from the cafeteria. No doubt what he'd been doing for the past month or so. He stopped trying after getting into a fight with Kai one night. That might've been a month or a month and a half ago. It was hard to remember when the days blurred together.

My body didn't like the walking, and I let out a breath when I finally reached the top of the building. The plan was to start from the top and work my way down. I'd learned in the past that he sometimes left notes on the table of where he might be.

The elevator dinged when I left, and I blinked back tears at the sight of the lonely waiting room. Ducking my head, I walked toward Avi's office and froze in the doorway when I found him.

Avi was asleep on the couch in his office, and my heart broke all over again when I saw how thin he'd gotten. There were several empty bottles of whiskey, another habit he'd picked up that I couldn't break him from. The stress of trying to keep him alive was killing me. I sniffed, hugging myself in the dim light of the room. He'd closed all the blinds to get sleep, and I almost couldn't wake him because I didn't know when last he slept.

I kept my footsteps quiet as I padded over, but I couldn't stop the tears. So much had happened since we got married... what was it, four or five months ago? The betrayal, the baby, the depression. Yet looking at him now hurt more than it did that night we fought near the hunting cabin. I don't even know when I realized how much I cared for Avi, but the words still stuck in my throat before I could say them.

We were going to have a baby, yet we were stuck between strangers and lovers. Not even friends. Friends at least spoke to each other when things got rough like this.

There was a blanket on a nearby couch and I grabbed it, gently pulling it across Avi's frame as he slept. I'd talk to him when he woke, but I couldn't keep doing everything without him.

Turning toward the opposite couch, I sat down and watched him for hours, happy and sad that he was finally resting. Happy because there were so many nights that I waited up to make sure he was going to sleep, and sad because he didn't need me to remind him this time.

I was still watching him when he grumbled about the light I left on near the bar, cursing a headache that he no doubt had after drinking so much. He didn't know I was there, and I was content to just watch him. We could talk when he finally woke up for real.

My cell phone was in my hands when I heard him mutter my name, and my heart rate nearly stilled to a stop as I watched him. It was on silent just in case one of the others called, but I messaged them all earlier to let them know I would stay until he woke up.

"I'm sorry," he mumbled, hand searching for his phone. I watched him pick it up, bringing it to his face and he winced. I waited for him to click on my name and phone me, then tilted my head when I realized he was texting me instead.

Flicking my messaging app open, I waited, hoping to see what he wanted to say. The message came through, and I opened it, hearing my heart thudding in my ears.

Avi [7:48 *p.m.*]: I wish I was brave enough to let you go.

Chapter 16

Avi

M<small>Y HEAD WAS POUNDING</small> when I woke again, and I didn't even have the energy to do anything about it. The ceiling would have to be the witness to my misery, but after months of trying to save that stupid project, it's been taken away from me. The business was being taken away from me, but that wasn't even the worst part.

I fucked up.

Badly.

My best friends hated me. My wife was alone in the hospital. Or she was two weeks ago when she sent me the message. *Pregnant*, her last message said. One that I couldn't even respond to until twenty minutes ago because I was such a fucking idiot.

Then there was Heinrich. Grandfather. Not that he ever was one. I got an in-person visit from him this afternoon. His leukemia was terminal, they were moving him to special care and he had a lovely little nurse to run around after him.

For five years, Kai, Silas, Maya, and I were working to overthrow him. After decades of abuse, I finally got close and then everything toppled. It was all a chess game, *and he was still winning.*

This time it actually was my fault. I let my anger get the best of me, just like it always did and look who got hurt in the process. Mom. Kai. Silas. Maya. *Alisha.* Each one was another mistake for me to regret, but it was *her* that I hurt the most.

After Maya's confession, I threw myself into my work, trying to save a project that was crashing far too quickly for me to fix things. Alisha was there for every step, she stopped going to the shelter and started delegating more of her work to the assistant I hired her, spending her days in the office with me instead. She brought me food, made sure I ate it, and then pulled me away before the exhaustion became too numbing. I got so much work done because I knew that she was there in the background, making sure everything else wouldn't crash while I was busy.

Then the board started putting more pressure on me, and I didn't want her help because it was interfering. I actually thought I could save it. We started fighting over stupid shit, I started staying in the office because it was easier than the guilt of staying at home with a wife that I hadn't even taken on a proper date yet. A wife that was now carrying my kid.

I wouldn't blame her for hating me for that. I was no better than my grandfather after what he did to Maya.

The days might've blurred, but there were memories of Alisha in every one of them. Always waiting. Sleeping on this couch because I was too fucking stubborn to go home, cleaning up my lab and my desk, bringing food, forcing me to look after myself. I still remember when she left last Saturday. God, she was angry. I smiled bittersweetly. *Spitfire.* I can't believe that I actually thought I would divorce her. My heart ached at the thought. It would've been healthier for her than to live like this.

My phone started ringing, and I picked it up, hoping to see her name. Except... that wasn't my phone. *That wasn't my phone?*

I picked my head up off the couch, grimacing, and turned to look around. The staff weren't allowed up on this floor, not unless they were cleaners. There was too much confidential shit lying around. I froze the moment my feet were on the ground, spotting Alisha's form on the couch across from me.

She mumbled a protest, stretching an arm to pat around for her cell phone, and then sat up when she couldn't find it.

"Spitfire," I called, my voice soft, but she heard it. I know she did, her whole body tightened the way it used to when we first met. "Alisha."

She picked up her phone, answering it instead of me. "Hello?" I stared at her feeling lost as she murmured quietly, her fingers picking at the blanket that fell onto her lap.

"I know, Tal. I won't be long, I promise." She went quiet, mumbling something that her uncle wouldn't hear, but I did, and my mouth twitched at the words, "I accidentally fell asleep."

After she put the phone down, Alisha met my eyes, and I felt my heart drop when a tear tracked down her face.

"Alisha?"

Her eyes closed on a sob and panic had me stumbling from the couch and to her.

"Spitfire," I murmured gently, pulling her into my arms like that night when I realized I was her first. The night I swore I would be her last too if I could. "I'm sorry. I'm sorry, Alisha. Tell me what's wrong and I'll fix it."

Her body shook in my arms like she was breaking, and I climbed onto the couch and dragged her on my lap, hugging her tight while I waited for it to stop.

"I'm sorry," I whispered, laying a kiss on her forehead. "I'm sorry."

It was my fault; I didn't need her to tell me to know that it was.

Eventually, the sobs subsided, and her arms reached around me, hugging me as tightly as I held her.

"Tell me," I murmured pleadingly. "I'm sorry."

Just tell me what I did so that I can fix it.

"I found the papers," she finally whispered, her voice breaking against my neck. "You stopped looking at me, and I was worried it meant that you didn't want me anymore. Then I found the papers while clearing your desk last weekend." Her body shuddered in my arms as she started crying again. "Is that what you want, Avi?"

My eyes squeezed shut. The divorce papers I left in my drawer. I brought them in from the hunting cabin so that she wouldn't see them. I should've thrown them away, but I forgot.

"I'll sign it if you promise you'll stop hurting yourself. Was that why you stopped coming home?" she sobbed. "You should've s—*said* something, Avi. I read your message. Do you wish you could let me go? What the fuck does that even mean? I was trying to help you. Why did it take you so long to say something?"

"Alisha," I buried my face in her hair. She was giving me an easy way out which meant she read the message I sent twenty minutes ago. I'm such a fucking idiot. Has she been lying here this whole time wondering about it while I was worrying about a stupid headache?

"No!" she hit my chest, pushing away from me. "Answer me, Avi, what do you want? Because I know what I want. I want coffee dates with Maya, and bringing food up to the office while Kai and Silas are joking around. I want you! I want my husband to start looking after himself again. Eating and sleeping when you're supposed to instead of getting wasted in your office. I want you to look at me again—because you were always looking at me, even when you didn't want to admit it. Do you know how many times I caught you looking?"

My hands cup her cheeks, "I'm looking at you now."

And I was, just like every other time, but this time she was crying, looking at me like I broke her heart. *Because I did.*

"Why did you ever stop?" she whispered, heartbroken. My own heart shattered to try and match.

"Because I felt guilty," I answered her, my forehead dropping to meet hers. "I felt guilty because you were forced into marrying me." I smoothed her hair away from her face. "Then I felt guilty because I was acting like an asshole, and yet you were still there every step of the way. You never left me, and I couldn't look at you when I knew that you deserved better."

Alisha didn't respond and panic flickered through me when she pulled away. Was it too late? Had I lost her already?

"Let's go home," I croaked out, my eyes closing again. I hadn't gone home in a while, I couldn't not after Silas left but Alisha had been begging me over and over. I had to do something, I couldn't just sit and wait for her to decide she'd had enough. "Come."

I pulled myself up, swaying slightly, and then held my hand out to her. "Please, baby."

"Fine," she sighed, but the moment she stood up, her face whitened, and Alisha fainted.

An hour later, Alisha lay on a hospital bed, her arms folded and her gaze unfocused. The only time she'd stopped to say anything at all was when Talon brought her a teddy bear from the gift shop downstairs and informed her that he was contacting everyone to let them know what was going on. Once he left, she went back to ignoring me.

I paced the length of the room as we waited for the doctor, my whole body tensed as frustrated hopelessness battled with patience. "Why didn't you tell me that this keeps happening?"

Silence answered me. Surprise, surprise. I stifled a growl, pinching the bridge of my nose. Talon entered the room again, his gaze a glare that followed me around the room until he turned back toward Alisha. "Rosa and Lena are on their way with Silas. Are you sure you don't want us to fetch you any clothes? I spoke to the nurses outside and they're under the impression that if the doctor doesn't see an improvement in the next hour or so then you're staying here for the night."

"No," my wife answered, her voice brittle. "My blood pressure will go down. I'm not going to sleep here tonight."

He muttered something under his breath and then nodded before leaving the room again.

"Yes, you will," I warned after he left. Pulling a chair up to her bedside, I sat down heavily. Alisha ignored my presence, swiping her sweating forehead.

When she fainted earlier, I nearly lost it. Her weak body slumped against me was a horror I never thought I would have to feel, and panic clawed at my insides as I phoned the first person I could think of. It ended up being Kai, which was better than I thought because his job in security meant that medical assistance was just a call away. Time stretched as he arranged an ambulance to bring us to the hospital, and I was forced to wait, clutching her to me until they could place her on a stretcher and take her downstairs to the ambulance waiting in the underground parking.

Talon and Kai were right there when we strode downstairs, the car idling next to the ambulance and right before I climbed in, I noticed the blonde woman in the front seat. *Maya.*

My eyes squeezed shut even now. I should've noticed the signs, and maybe if I spoke up then she would've known better to fall for my grandfather's crap.

"Mr. and Mrs. Zohran," the doctor called, pulling me away from Alisha's side. "I've received the diagnostics." His voice sounded grim. I faced him, foreboding settling in my gut, the feeling only aided by Alisha's sudden stiffening.

"Is it serious?" was the first question that slipped out of my mouth, but I had to know.

The doctor's face was sympathetic. "Your wife has an extremely high blood pressure. We've tested her and she came back positive for symptoms of pre-eclampsia."

"What does that mean?" I asked as Alisha started to stir beside me.

"Your wife's blood pressure is extremely high; in fact, from what I can see on her personal records here... she was admitted less than two weeks ago for fainting due to the same problem. While fainting isn't abnormal for pregnancies, fainting due to blood pressure immediately puts your wife at risk for pre-eclampsia during her birth. We've taken the necessary steps to ensure her blood pressure lowers in the next hour or two, but your wife will remain a high-risk patient until she gives birth, and possibly even afterward. If left untreated, there will be a high likelihood of fatality in both the mother and her unborn child."

The blood rushed from my face. Fatality? "You think she won't survive the birth?" I choked out and my gaze immediately went to Alisha again. All the stress she'd been under, all the stress that I *put her under* led to this.

The doctor continued in his explanation and Alisha stared me down the entire time, stubbornness in the tilt of her chin told me she wasn't surprised by this most recent event.

"In cases like these," the doctor started to fidget, his fingers shifting the knot on his tie before he cleared his throat and tried again. "That is, while I understand it's a very difficult decision to make, sometimes in cases like these it's recommended that the pregnancy be terminated to avoid risking the health of the mother."

"We're not doing that," Alisha hissed, her eyes sparking with rage. The heart rate monitor beside her started to beep unevenly, almost frantically.

"Alisha," I murmured, reaching for her hand.

"No, Avi!" she snapped, but I continued, interlocking my fingers with hers.

"I'm sorry," I turned toward the doctor. "Is it possible for us to have a moment to talk?"

He nodded, leaving the room quietly and closing the door behind himself. As soon as we were alone, I turned toward Alisha, but she spoke before I could.

"I won't get an abortion, Avi." Her tone drew my attention.

"How long have you known about this?" I asked instead, clasping her hand between both of mine even though she kept it limp.

"Since the Saturday I left you," she muttered in a barely audible voice. "The doctor recommended the same thing then."

Desperate, I drew her fingers toward my mouth for a kiss and was awarded with a sharp intake of breath. "I'm not going to make you do something you don't want to do, Alisha, but I would like to discuss it."

"What is there to discuss," she bit out, with-drawing her hand. I let her and leaned back into my chair. At least her eyes were on me now, at least I had a bit of her attention. Maybe things weren't over just yet. "It's my body."

I agreed, but my mouth thinned at the thought of losing her. "And you're my wife."

She scoffed. "You say that, Avi, but the divorce papers in your drawer say something else en-tirely."

My eyes closed and I let out a sigh. "You should've told me when you found them, Alisha."

"*Really*," she drawled. "And when was I sup-posed to do that, Avi? When you were answer-ing my phone calls? My messages? You've been working non-stop since what happened with Maya, and every time I try to talk then you find another excuse."

I grimaced, attempting to reach for her hands again but she pulled them away from my grip. "No, I'm not done," Alisha warned, her voice cracking. "I *know* that our marriage is nothing more than an obligation. I *know* that the busi-ness is important, but I honestly thought that these past few months changed things."

"They have," I argued and this time when I went to pick up her hand, she let me. "I was wrong, okay. I was wrong for ignoring you, and I was wrong for telling you that you are nothing more than an obligation. When we met, you were terrified and I thought it would be easier if I let you hate me rather than trying because I *did* want a divorce, Alisha. I never would've married you if I had a choice in it."

She ripped her hand away, a sob catching in her throat, and I shook my head, feeling the same pain in my heart that I saw in her eyes.

"When we met, we were both signing an agreement because of bad blood created when my father married my mother instead of your aunt," I reminded her, my hand stretching until I could touch the closest part of her. It turned out to be her knee, and I squeezed it reassuringly.

"You told me that already," she muttered hoarsely.

"Yes," I admitted. "But I didn't get a chance to tell you the rest. A few years ago, I went looking for my mother. I've lived with my grandfather my whole life, but we were never close, and he refused to answer any questions I had about her. After an old friend of my father's commented how much she hated giving me up, I decided to look for her just to find out what was the truth. Kai and Silas were with me the whole time, and the things we found out changed my opinion about my grandfather entirely. He forced her to give me up, Alisha. Threatened me, threatened *her*. She stayed with me for a whole year, though most people assumed she had left right after the birth. However, that wasn't the case. In our searches for her, we came across multiple cases of abuse against my grandfather, things he paid others to cover up. There was evidence of each encounter he had with her, evidence that was sickening to see but worse than all of that was the evidence that my grandfather had on file. He had her committed to several rehabilitation centers, and because he had money it was easy enough to pay the right people off. She ran away out of pure desperation, and I can't hold that against her, but I did hold it against *him*."

"Maya," Alisha croaked out, tears in her eyes. I nodded.

"She didn't know. We couldn't say anything to anyone in case it would alert him. The plan was to take away everything of his. The company, his money... but he held it all over my head and changed his will to make sure that I couldn't get a cent without first doing what he wanted—"

"Marrying me," Alisha finished for me, and I nodded.

"He found out about the leukemia while we were still setting our plans into motion, it caused a lot of complications and I was forced to play along until we could complete the plan, but then the information leaks and break-ins started happening," I explained irritably. "I don't blame Maya for what she did, not when my plan had been to do the same thing. I just wish she had been more forthcoming. We would've stood by her if she had."

"You should've stood by her when she explained." Maya's eyes narrowed, and I nodded my head.

"I know, but the plan had been to take everything away from him, not to lose it." I regretted how things happened, but I still supported Maya's case against my grandfather, and I made sure that no one pressed any charges. "I've been in touch with Lena since Maya's confession," I admitted, and Alisha's eyes widened. "I know that you've been helping her, and I wanted to make sure that she had the required documents to sue him. However, I couldn't publicly back her without losing the support of the board and I still needed that to continue with the project."

"You're still planning to take over the company," she guessed, and I nodded.

"Yes, I am... or I *was*," I rectified quietly.

"What does that mean?" Alisha questioned and I shook my head.

"It means that I'm not going to do anything that will risk you," I said simply, my fingers tracing a pattern on her leg. Alisha stiffened at my words, and I turned to look at her.

"Avi," she started, and her brow furrowed as she leaned in to grab my hand. I glanced at her questioningly as she settled it on the almost unnoticeable bump. "I'm not going to give up my baby."

My laugh was brittle, and I leaned my forehead against her knees. "I can't lose you."

"Then do I have your support in this," she asked, an eyebrow raised defiantly.

I searched her eyes, seeing nothing but determination there and I sighed. "I won't lose you," I repeated. "I know it hasn't been easy but I'm willing to do anything to make it up to you."

"Avi." she reached out and caressed my cheek. The way her breath caught made my name sound like a goodbye and I shook my head.

"Let's just take things slow," I whispered. "One thing at a time until we get it right."

A tear dropped down her face, but she nodded in agreement. That was all I needed and before we called the doctor back in, I vowed to make her fall in love with me properly this time.

Epilogue

Alisha

THE LIGHTS OUTSIDE MY apartment window comforted me once more, and I hugged my knees close as I stared at the city below. A year ago, I had sat staring at this same view before my wedding, wondering where my life would be and how things would end up.

Avi's arms around me were a comfort, I was still recovering from my difficult pregnancy and birth, but he'd been there, and our relationship had only gotten stronger. The grief of what could've been no longer bothered me and that was all because of him. He was my strength and I appreciated him more every day because of it.

"What a day," Avi murmured, leaning into our embrace.

"Mhmm." I agreed. Maya had won her court case against his grandfather today and we all celebrated with champagne in the city. I never dreamed of a family like this, but now that I had it, I wouldn't give it up for anything.

We were still working on a plan to vindicate his mother and Maya by taking the company away from Heinrich Zohran, but that didn't matter right then, and I had another thing in my mind as I turned from the windows.

"Avi," I started to say before he interrupted me with a kiss.

"Wait," he broke away, a dazzling grin on his face as he pulled out something from his pocket. A ring box? I raised an eyebrow in question, and he kissed me once more before pulling away.

"Now that we have some time," he began as he dropped to one knee. "I wanted to make my intentions known."

I snorted out a laugh, dropping on my knees as well. "What are you doing, you fool? We're already married." I ruffled his hair and kissed his cheek, my belly aching as more laughter poured out of me.

"No," Avi interrupted, and I raised an eyebrow as he opened the ring box. "The night you were in the hospital, I promised to make things right. I also promised to make you fall in love with me again, so this time I want to ask you for myself. Will you, Alisha Zohran, allow me the pleasure to make you fall in love with me for the rest of my life?"

A grin was fighting to break through, twisting my lips. "And if I already do love you, Avi Zohran?"

He blinked, "You love me."

"Every stubborn and annoyingly gorgeous part of you," I declared, swinging my arms around his neck.

"Then marry me again, anyway," he murmured against my lips. "I love you, spitfire, but I want to do this right." He pulled away and cleared his throat, the ring box held out toward me. "Tell me, spitfire. Will you marry me again, properly this time?"

Amara, my little miracle, cooed nearby and a smile came to my lips as I tipped my head back. No, I would never trade this for anything.

"Yes. I will marry you," I kissed him. "I will marry you a thousand times, Avi, but I won't change a thing because it gave us *her*."

He grinned, facing our daughter. The daughter we'd come so close to losing. My Amara.

The End...

"Hold onto your hearts! The next ride is about to begin.

Get a glimpse of my upcoming book..."

Baby With My Brother's Best Friend: An Age Gap, Enemies To Lovers Romance

A one-night stand, with a hot older man. Just my luck, he's my brother's best friend!

I just wanted a night of fun, letting down my hair and breaking all my rules.

In walks 6ft tall, sun-kissed skin, smoking-hot eyes, and perfect lips. He was just what the Dr. ordered.

I needed to break free of my good girl rut and oh did he break me!

Fast forward, I'm set to meet my brother for a business meeting when walking in...

I was struck with the same dark eyes and luscious lips of that blissful night. Mr. one night stand!

My brother introduced him as his best friend Tyler, to my surprise, his eyes were cold and distant.

I can't believe he forgot our night!

Fine! if that's how he wants to play it. Thanks for the night.

There's only one problem.

I missed my period.

Ready for more? Check out the 1st Chapter...

Chapter 16

Mia

THIS IS THE FIRST time I've been to a club like this since I've been in San Diego, something utterly unheard of, seeing as I spent four years here attending college. Although I returned to Colombia right after college and spent almost a year living with my large family, I came right back to San Diego a month ago.

After moping around from missing my family and how I left things with them before moving back to this city and much pleading from my best friend, Polly, I finally dragged myself out of my room and agreed to go to a club with her.

Tonight, I've made up my mind not to think about any of the drama I left back in Colombia. Nor will I think about the fact that in this twenty-first century, my parents think they can just pick out a man for me to marry and have babies with.

For the first time in my twenty-five years of life, I'm not going to be the good, obedient girl who always does what her parents tell her. I will be wild, carefree Mia, who is finally making her own path in this world, without worrying about the consequences or the disappointed look on her parents' face.

"Are you ready for the best night of your life, girl?" Polly grins, swinging her long red hair from side to side while her blue eyes sparkle brightly with excitement.

I first met Polly back in my first year at college. We had been taking an elective course together, and it didn't matter that we had two completely different personalities. We immediately clicked. Her lifestyle intrigued me, especially how she impulsively did things just because she could.

Oftentimes, I envied how she lived by her rules and hers alone. She lived every single day like it was her last, and I plan on doing the same this time around. No more nice, good girl Mia.

That girl was dead and buried.

"Hell yes," I pump my fist into the air. "I'm ready to activate Mia 2.0."

We grab each other's hands, swinging them along as we head towards the bouncer who quickly lets us in after Polly slips a dollar into his front pocket and winks at him. I suspect the two are either having or used to have a thing. I can't exactly keep up with Polly's love life.

As soon as we step inside the club, it's like I've been entirely transported into a new world. The space is decorated in such a way that dark leather chairs are arranged in a curve while a glass-encased stage stands in the middle for the strippers to perform. The bar counter is at the end of the room and from the corner of my eyes, I can see the muscled bartender performing shirtless tricks much to the delight of the giggling ladies that surround him.

The ceiling is beautified with a large, layered chandelier that dispels several neon lights from purple to green to pink to blue and orange. On the far right-hand side is the DJ area where a fair-headed man with headphones around his neck mixes and matches songs that gets the audience dancing.

I'm pretty sure my mouth drops in awe and intrigue as I watch different couples grind against each other on the dance floor. One in particular looks like they're about to have sex right there on the spot.

Blushing, I quickly look away and my eyes land on one of the chairs in the corner. That's when I see him.

Dark, brooding eyes that speak volumes of dangerous yet pleasurable promises, watching me with clear interest and desire. His thick lips call to me and I briefly wonder what they would taste like.

There are light stubbles scattered across his jaw as if he hasn't had the time to shave yet. He has on a black shirt and black trousers. Judging from the way he looked, it's easy to tell that beneath his clothing is an impressive body. He has left the two top buttons open and it offers me a teasing glimpse of his glistening bronze chest.

I don't know how long I stand there, gaping openly at him. He looks oddly familiar, but I can't quite place where I met him from.

I'm still trying to decipher where I could have possibly met this incredibly gorgeous man from when he stands and strides toward me. Before I know it, he's standing right in front of me.

"You seem like you want a lot of things, princess. Tell me one and I'll make it happen."

His baritone voice reverberates through my entire body, leaving me boneless and unable to resist its hold on me.

I gulp.

I looked around trying to be sure that this man was actually talking to me. I also noticed to my dismay, Polly was nowhere to be seen. I could have sworn she was right next to me when we walked in earlier.

"If you're looking for your friend, she's over there." he pointed me right to where Polly was, and I wasn't even surprised to see her giggling with a bartender.

Great. She had ditched me for drinks.

"Thank you very much for pointing that out". I wanted him to go away already. I'll admit, the earlier confidence I was feeling was starting to dwindle.

But really, was I going to just allow my resolve to falter just because Polly wasn't here right now to edge me on?

Forcing my confidence in myself, I walked closer to him and placed my hands on either side of his shoulders. I could see the glimmer of excitement in his dark eyes, I couldn't quite tell the exact shade his eyes were because of the lights that kept flickering but I could see one thing in his eyes, he wanted to know my next move.

"I believe you asked me a question a few minutes ago," I smiled, angling my head to the side so a little of my neck could be seen. This was the first time I was coming on strong to a guy. I always waited for men to make the first move.

But tonight? Tonight was the start of Mia living her life for her. Not for anyone else.

"Yes, I did"

"Wonderful." I leaned in close to his right ear and whispered, "Ask me again," before pulling away and meeting his gaze with equal lust. We both knew where this was headed, and I didn't back down.

He didn't look like a coward either. The perfect match if you ask me.

"You seem like you want a lot of things, princess. Tell me one, and I'll make it happen."

I laughed.

"Why don't we get out of here and you fuck me," I stated

We were both adults, there was no use beating around the bush. I wanted this just as much as he did. The sooner we got it out of our system, the better.

"I thought you would never ask," he smiled

"Just give me a second. I have to inform my friend," he smiled as I walked away.

"Polly", I tapped her shoulders, standing behind her. She gave me a warm smile and embraced me.

"It's Mia! My friend." She smiled at me and I rolled my eyes. She was almost making me rethink my earlier decision. Was I going to just leave her here like this when it seemed like she was struggling to remember my name?

"You have had too much to drink. We need to get you home." I gripped her wrists and walked the both of us back to the hunk I was talking to earlier.

"We will leave right after I drop her off at home. Do you have a car?."

"Yes, I do," he smiled.

"Look at thattt. It's a cute guy and oh my, he's touching me", Polly giggled as He tried to steady her so we could take her out of the club.

Thankfully, we got Polly out of the club in one piece and his car was parked very close to the entrance so it wasn't so difficult getting her into the car.

I knew it was very unsafe that I was telling my address to a man I had just met a few minutes ago but right now, it was the best shot I had. I couldn't risk anything happening to Polly.

We arrived at my house in less than fifteen minutes and he helped me carry Polly upstairs.

"You can wait here while I tuck her into bed."

He looked very out of place in our living room but at the same time, I had to remind myself that this was just a one-night thing. I just needed to release all the tension.

"Hey. Handle me gently!", Polly yelled at me as I placed her on the bed. I really felt like slapping some sense into her right now. If she hadn't completely drank herself to stupor, I would probably be on my third orgasm tonight right now.

"Just shut up and sleep."

"I know what you're going to do after you leave me here. Just please use protection!" she yelled, and I gasped

I hoped he hadn't heard that. I tucked Polly into my bed, shut off her lights, and walked to the living room.

"I'm so sorry about her. I just had to make sure she was okay." I smiled. "Should? we head out now?" I asked him, and instead of saying anything, he smiled and walked towards me. I could see that he had a challenging look in his eyes, which ran shivers down my spine.

"I have to be at a project early tomorrow, so how about we do it here? Me and you. I'm guessing you live here too, and you have a room?" he asked me, placing a light kiss on my shoulder blade.

Oh. My. Goodness.

If I didn't get a hold of something right now, I felt like I would actually fall because my legs had suddenly turned to mush.

"But my friend would be in the next room," I whispered. He wrapped one hand right around my waist, placing more kisses from my neck down to my shoulders.

"I doubt she would", he smiled. He gave me a playful wink before claiming my lips.

It's official. I was wet.

I couldn't explain what this man was doing to me but it was nothing like I had ever felt before. I loved the way he was kissing me and I never wanted it to end. If this was what wilding and finding my own path felt like, then I was all up for it for tonight. In one swift movement, he lifted me off the floor, and I wrapped my legs around his thigh.

"Where's your room?" he asked me between kisses, but I could hear exactly what he meant.

"That way", I responded, kissing him with equal passion. We reached my room in seconds because of his long strides. He shut the door behind him with his leg and threw me on the bed. I didn't even have enough time to recover from that when he towered over me, pulling my dress down with a smirk on his face.

He slid my panties off me and before I could say Jack, he had slipped one finger inside me. I was extremely wet right now and I could feel it.

"Oh", I moaned.

He shook his head and covered my lips with his free hand

"We don't want to alert your friend, remember?", he winked and I nodded like a little child

"That's a good girl", he added slipping another finger into me. I threw my head back on the board of my bed. He gave me a wicked grin and slipped his hands out of my wet fold. Without breaking eye contact with me he moved his hands to his nose, inhaling my juices before licking both fingers that had my juices. My vision darkened and I was so aroused by this. He had tasted my juices.

He smiled and pushed me lower on the bed, placing one of my pillows on my back before looking up at me.

"I'm about to take you on a ride of your life baby girl. I need you to not scream. Are we good?", I nodded.

I couldn't wait for what he wanted to do to me and I could feel my vagina throbbing erratically. I reached my hands to my lower area and tried to touch it because I could feel myself growing impatient, but he pushed my hands away.

In one swift motion, he spread my thighs far apart from each other before dipping his head in between my thighs and licking my folds.

"Ahhhh. Ohhhh", I almost moaned but I had to bite back my screams. This wasn't the first time I was being eaten out, but he was doing it with so much expertise that he had my thighs buckling in seconds, and my first orgasm hit me in waves.

"We are just getting started." he smiled and took off his shirt.

By the time he was done taking off his clothes, I gasped when I saw how thick his shaft was. I gulped and reached forward for him, taking his member in my mouth. He pushed his head back and held on to my head as I sucked him with so much intensity. This was the best sexual feeling I had ever felt. He groaned before he pushed me down again on the bed and spread my thighs wide before settling in between them.

"Try not to scream," he teased.

" I won't." I was already growing impatient and needy, and I just needed him inside me already. "Just fuck me already."

"As you wish," he winked, then he entered me in one sharp movement. My mouth curved into an "O" shape as he gave me the best fuck of my life that night.

Enjoyed this sneak peek?
Click here to grab your free copy of
Baby With My Brother's Best Friend: An Age Gap, Enemies To Lovers Romance

Made in the USA
Middletown, DE
09 September 2024

60075586R00167